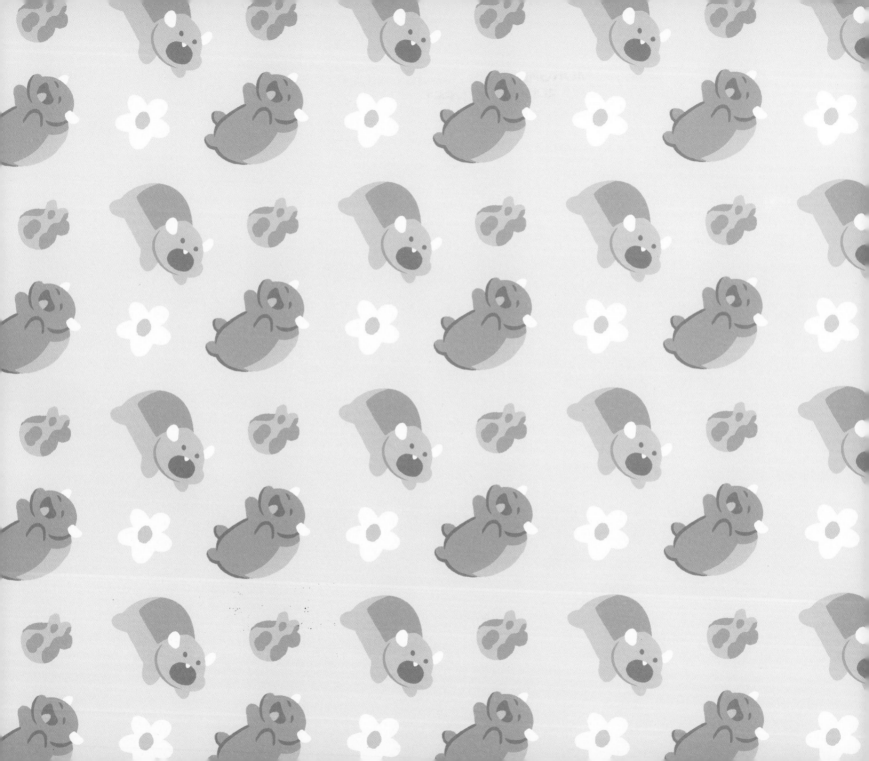

Lost Beast, Found Friend

ONI PRESS

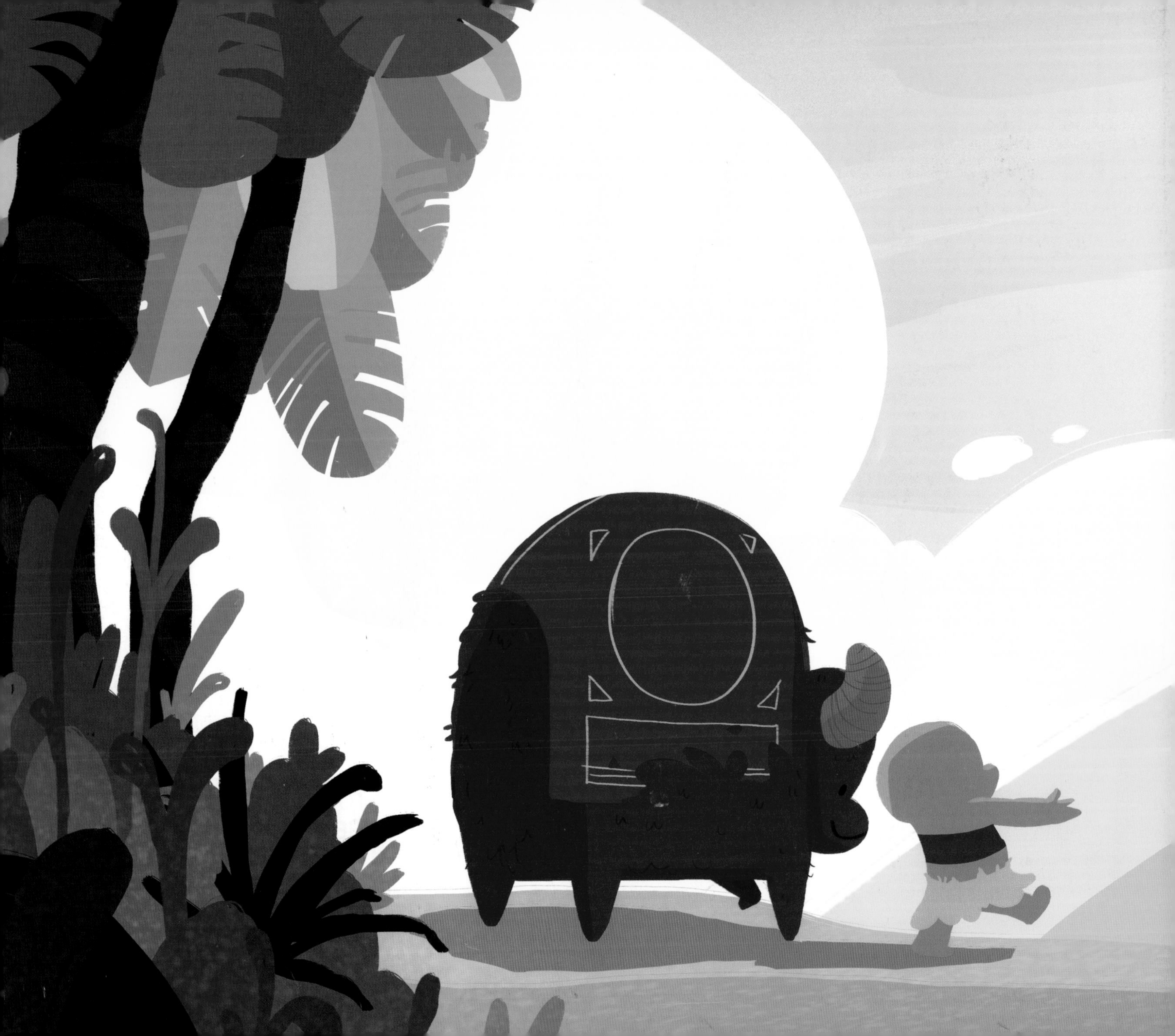

Lost Beast, Found Friend

NICK KENNEDY and JOSH TRUJILLO

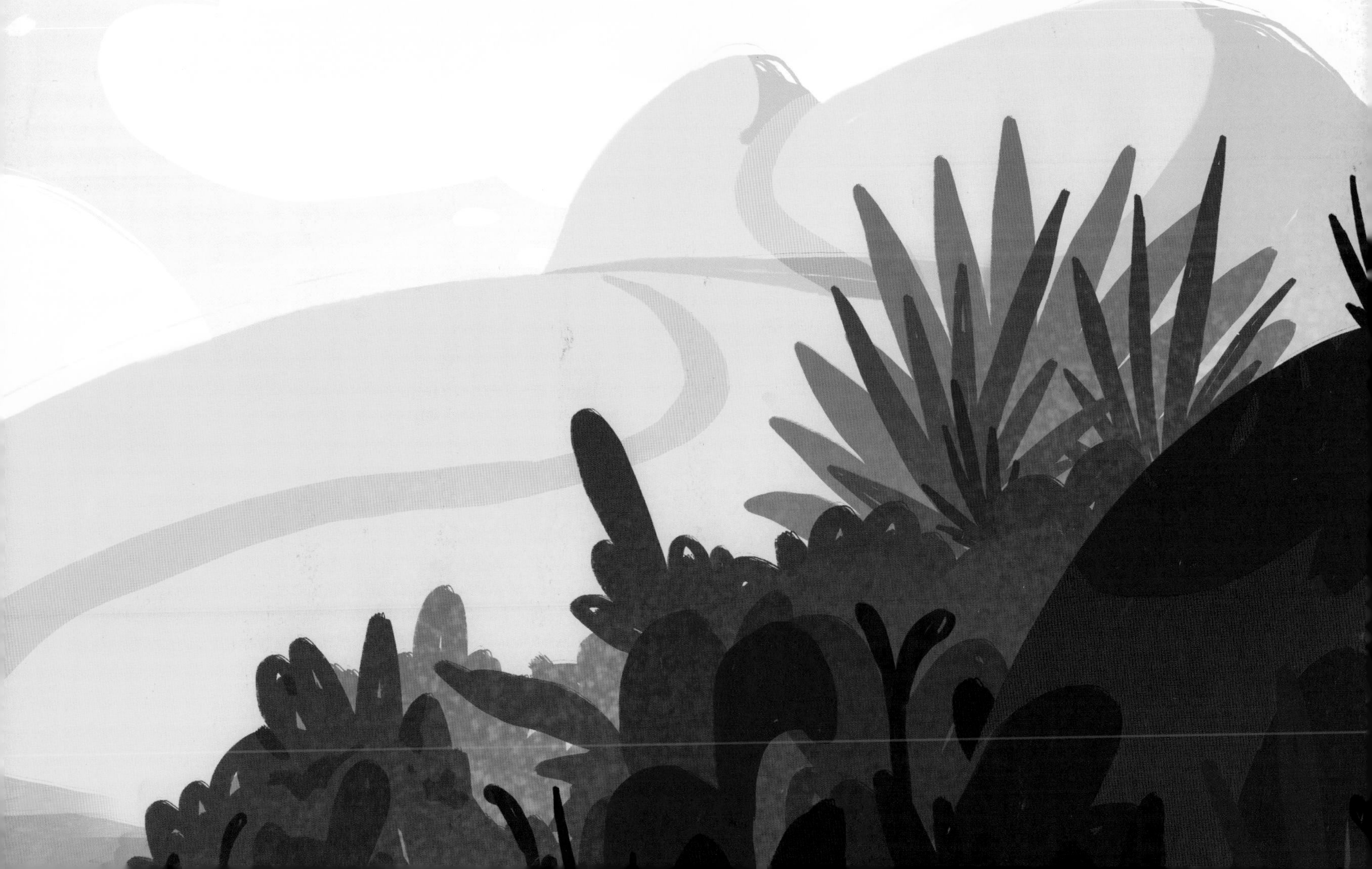

Illustrated by **Nick Kennedy**
Written by **Josh Trujillo**
Designed and lettered by **Melanie Lapovich**
Edited by **Christina "Steenz" Stewart**
Additional editing assistance by **Grace Bornhoft**

paintwithnick.net
joshtrujillo.com

PUBLISHED BY ONI-LION FORGE PUBLISHING GROUP, LLC

James Lucas Jones, president & publisher • Sarah Gaydos, editor in chief • Charlie Chu, e.v.p. of creative & business development • Brad Rooks, director of operations • Amber O'Neill, special projects manager • Harris Fish, events manager • Margot Wood, director of marketing & sales • Jeremy Atkins, director of brand communications • Devin Funches, sales & marketing manager • Katie Sainz, marketing manager • Tara Lehmann, marketing & publicity associate • Troy Look, director of design & production • Kate Z. Stone, senior graphic designer • Sonja Synak, graphic designer • Hilary Thompson, graphic designer • Sarah Rockwell, junior graphic designer • Angie Knowles, digital prepress lead • Vincent Kukua, digital prepress technician • Shawna Gore, senior editor • Robin Herrera, senior editor • Amanda Meadows, senior editor • Jasmine Amiri, editor • Grace Bornhoft, editor • Zack Soto, editor • Steve Ellis, vice president of games • Ben Eisner, game developer • Michelle Nguyen, executive assistant • Jung Lee, logistics coordinator

Joe Nozemack, publisher emeritus

onipress.com | lionforge.com
facebook.com/onipress | facebook.com/lionforge
twitter.com/onipress | twitter.com/lionforge
instagram.com/onipress | instagram.com/lionforge

FIRST EDITION: JUNE 2020

ISBN 978-1-62010-742-3 • eISBN 978-1-62010-746-1

Library of Congress Control Number: 2019955385

1 2 3 4 5 6 7 8 9 10

We dedicate this book to our friendship.
Making something special takes a lot of work,
so it helps to have a great friend by your side.

- Nick and Josh

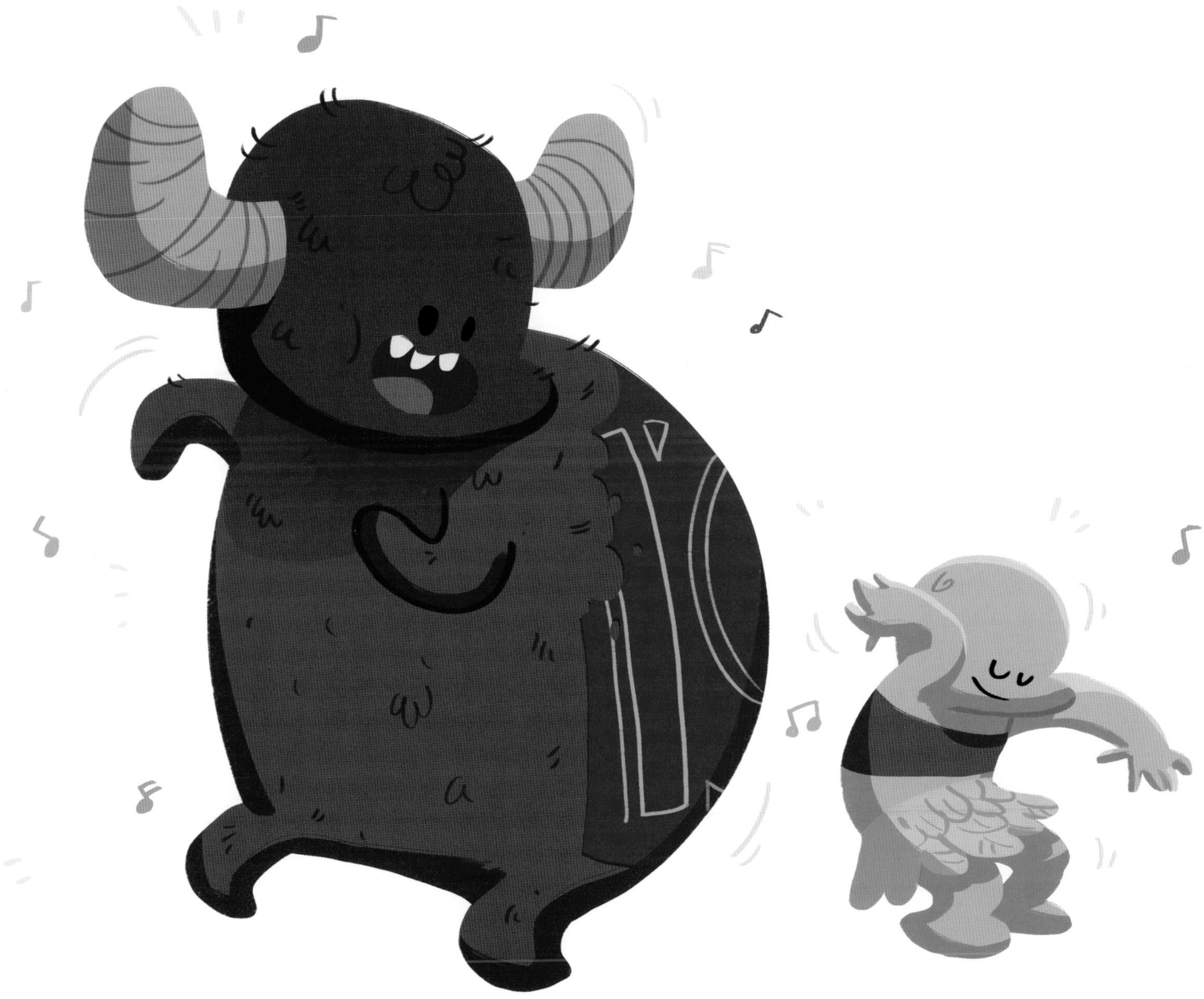

In a village by the sea,
lived the island girl
Keelee.

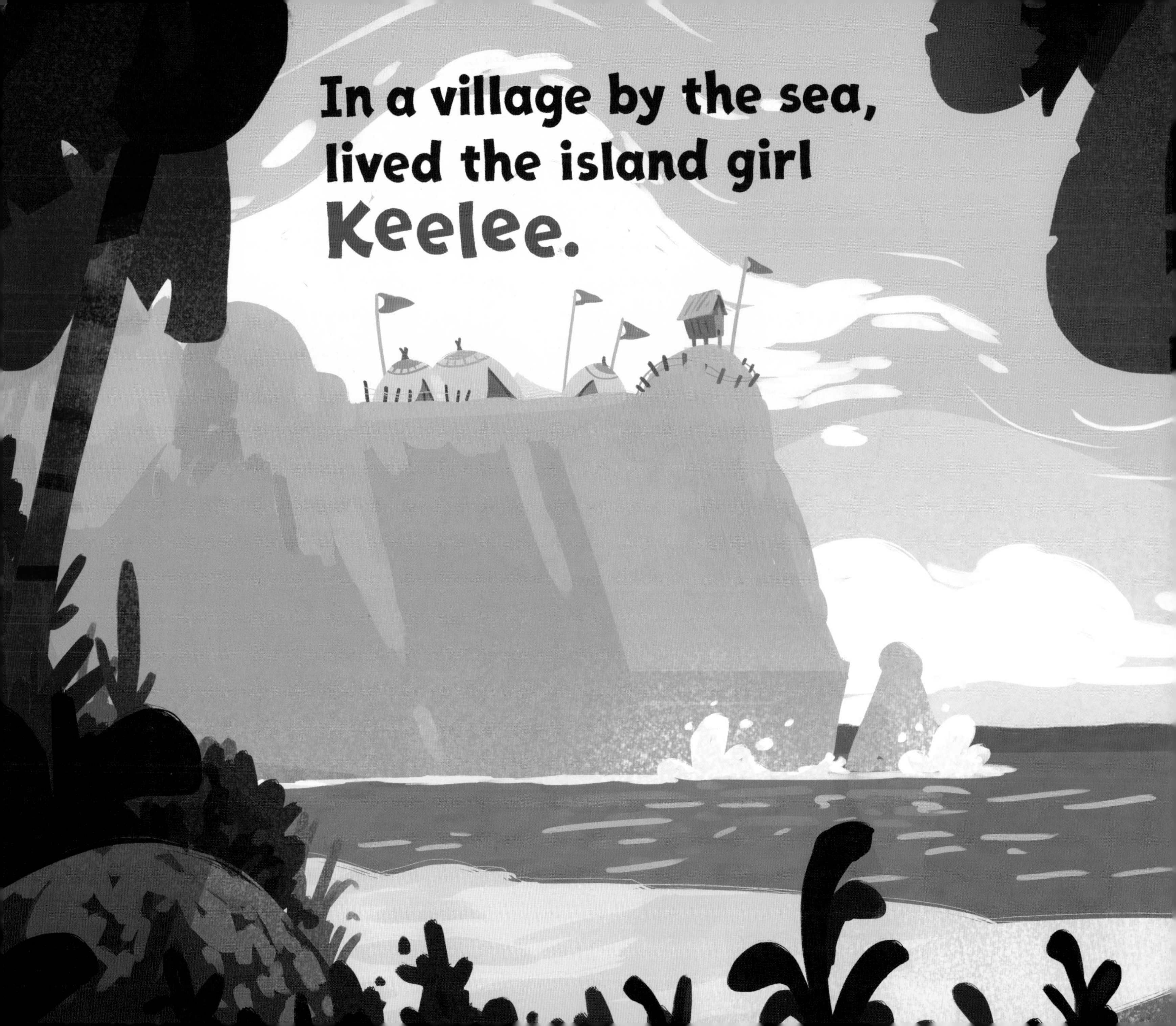

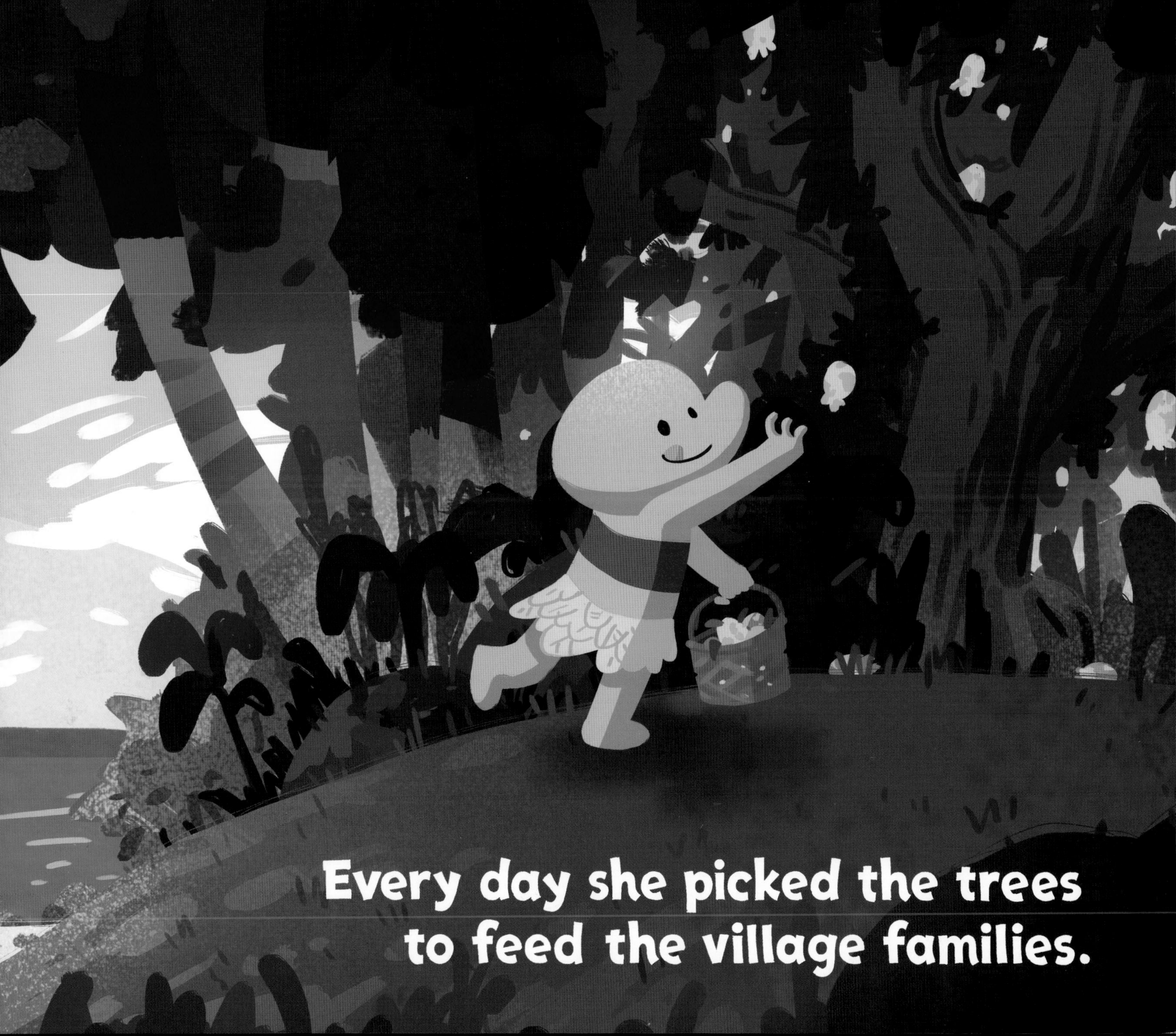

Every day she picked the trees
to feed the village families.

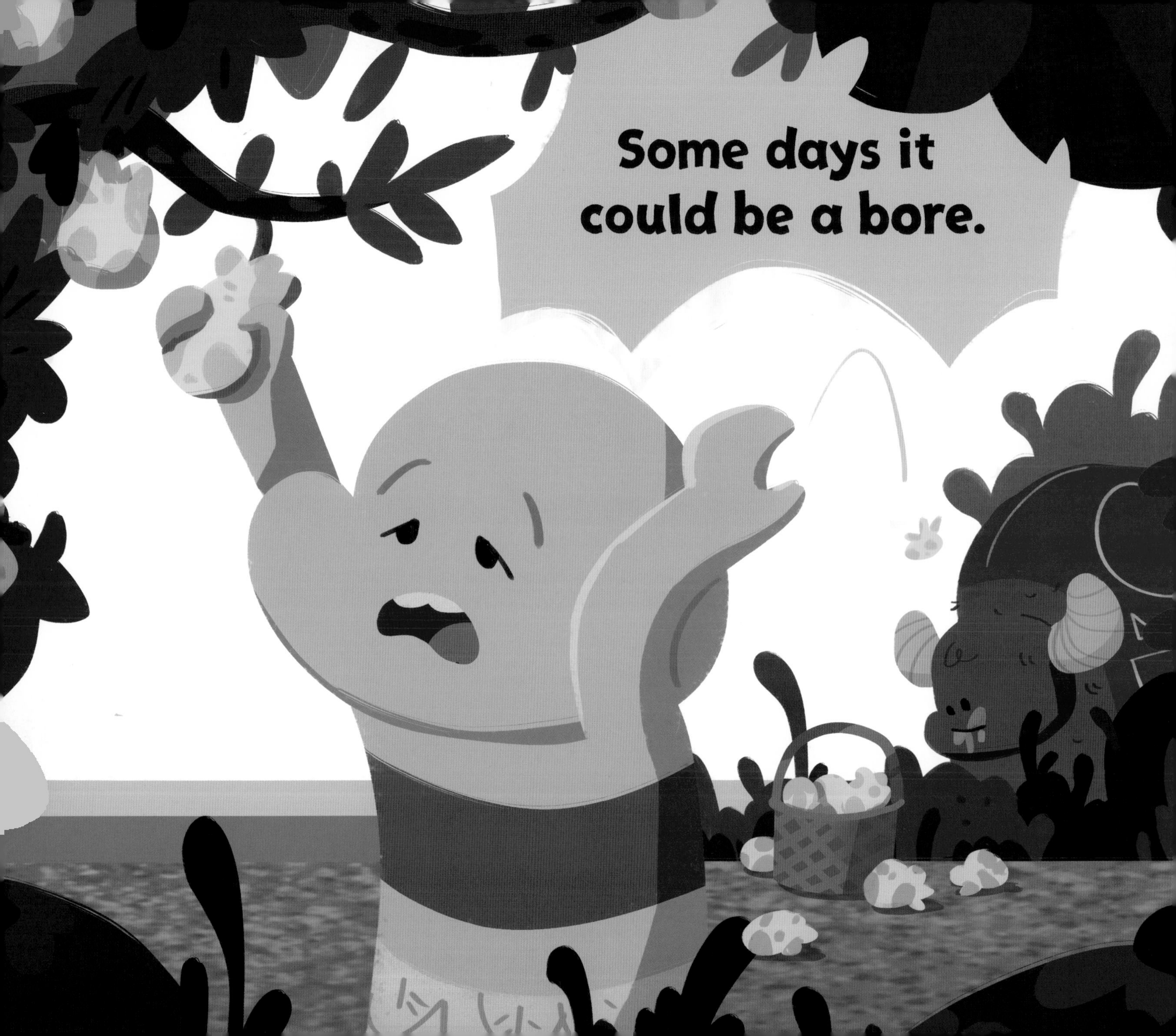

Some days it could be a bore.

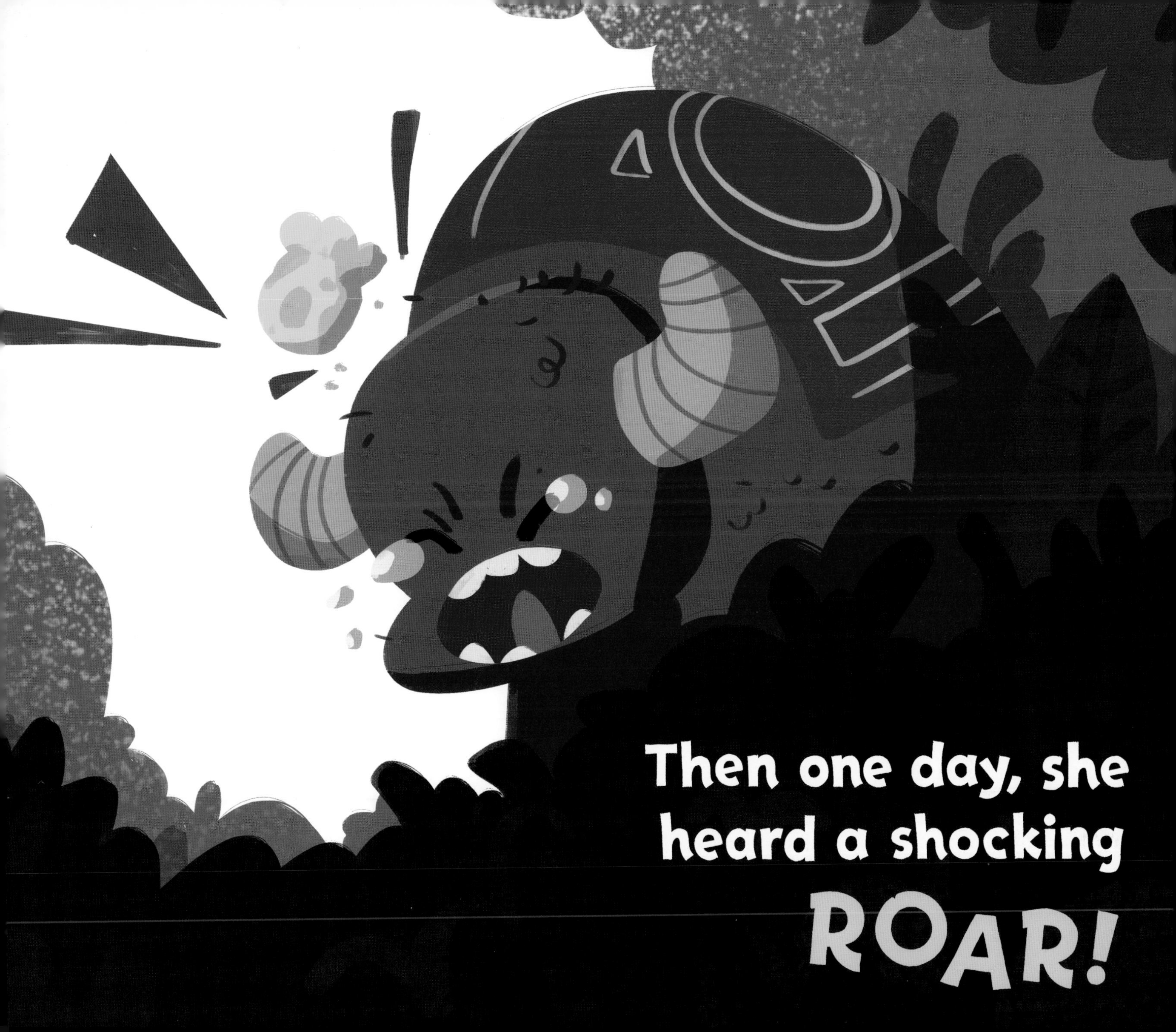

Then one day, she heard a shocking

ROAR!

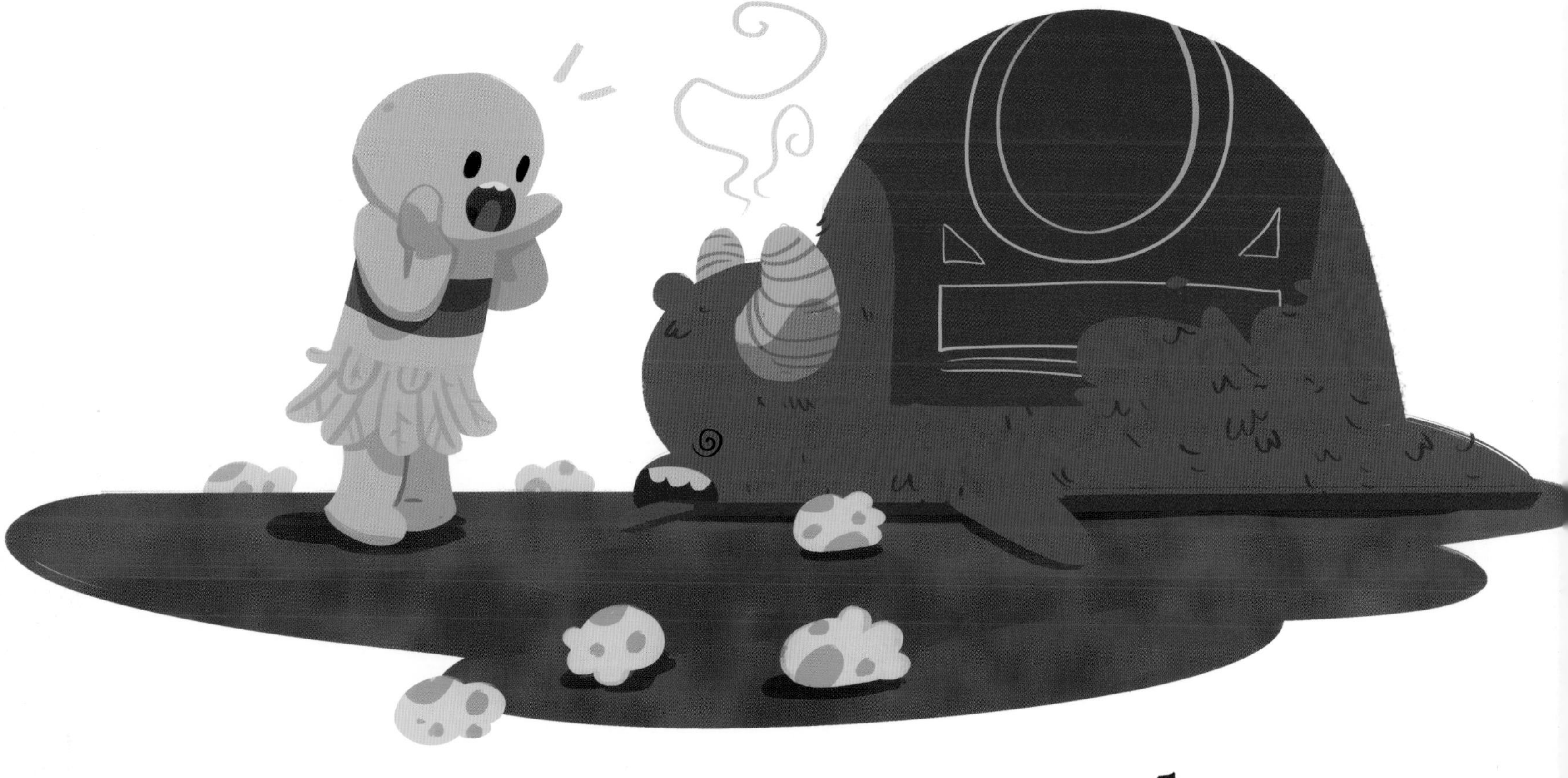

Purple, fuzzy...

...on all fours...

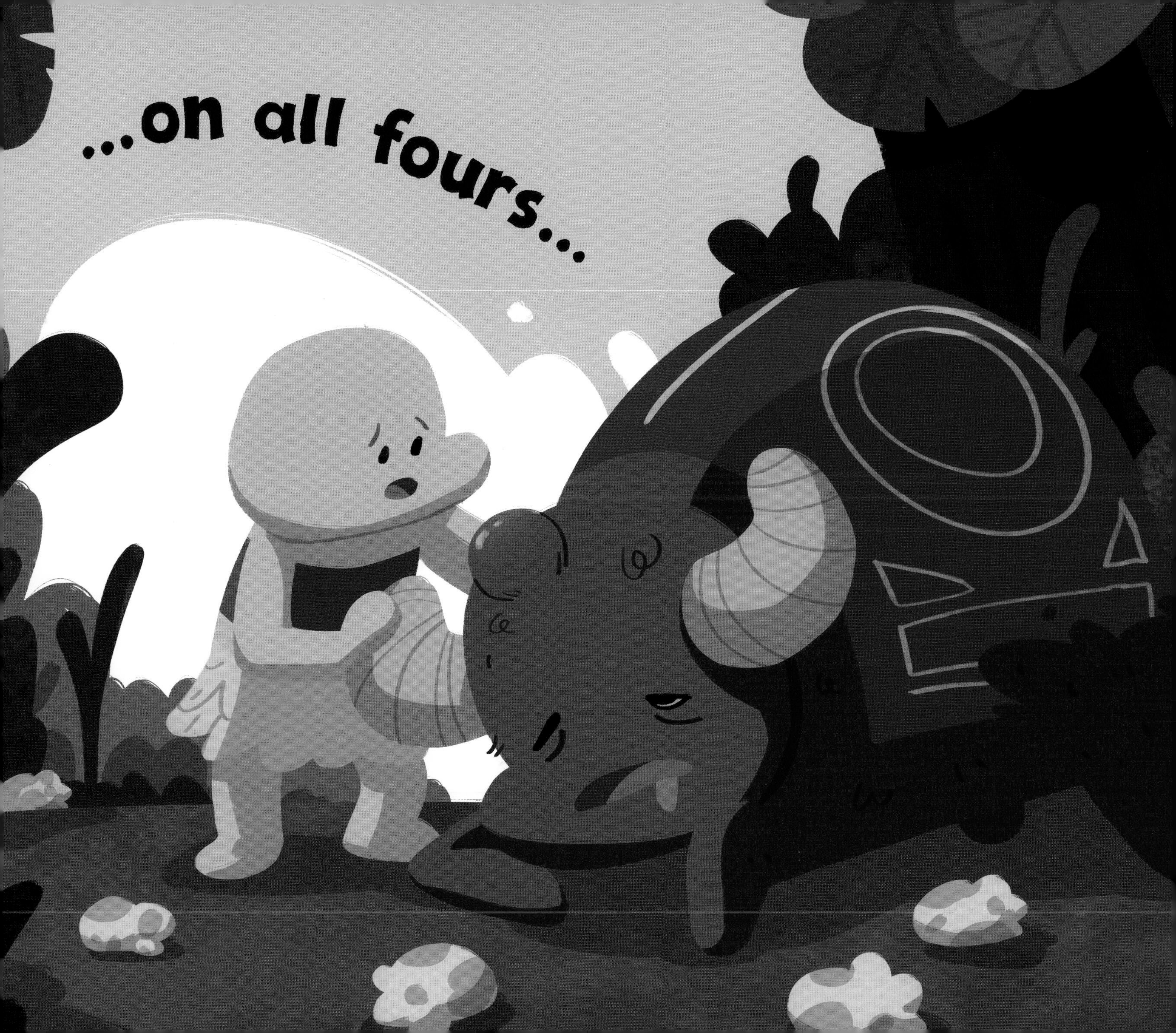

She'd never
seen anything
like it before!

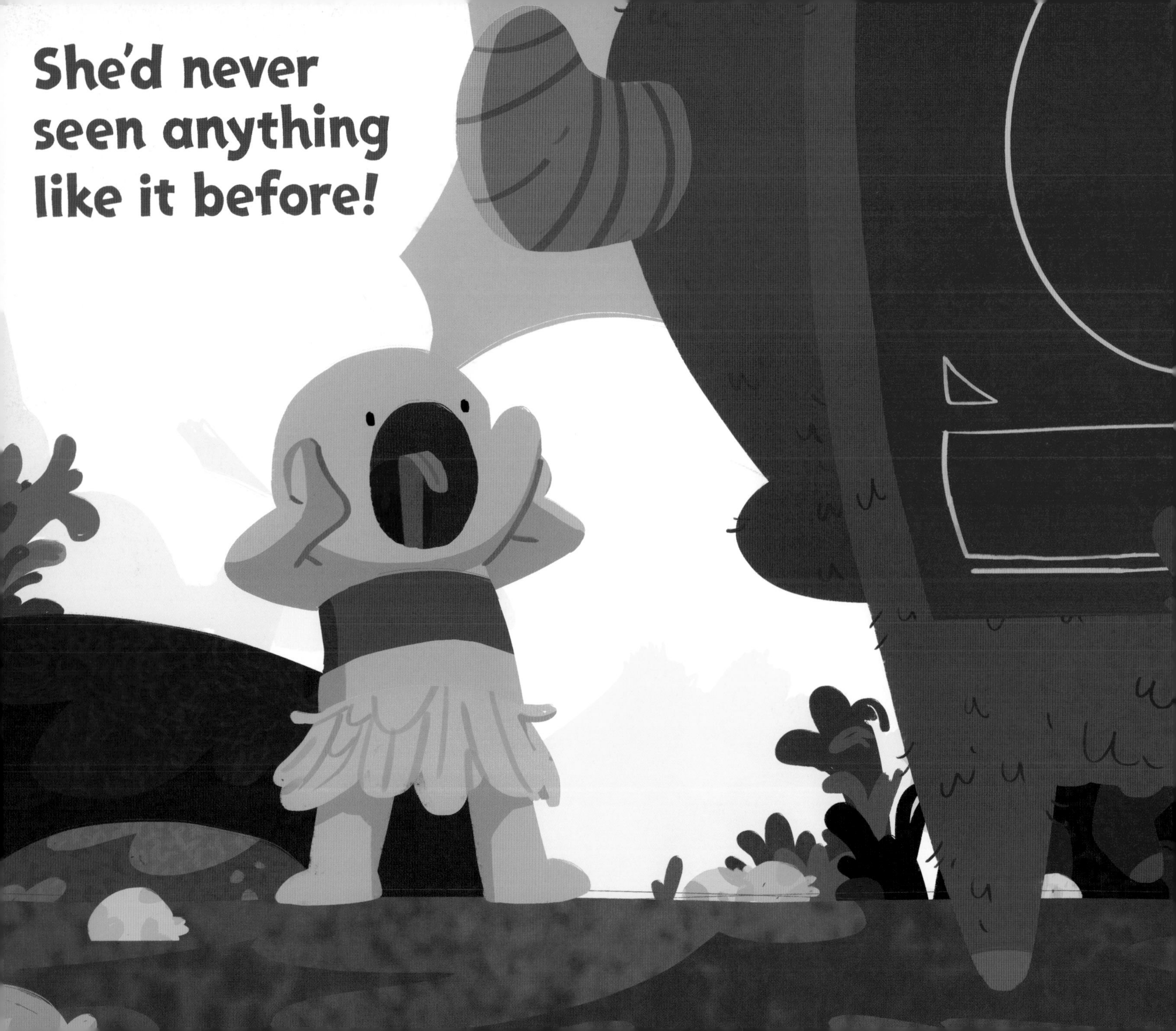

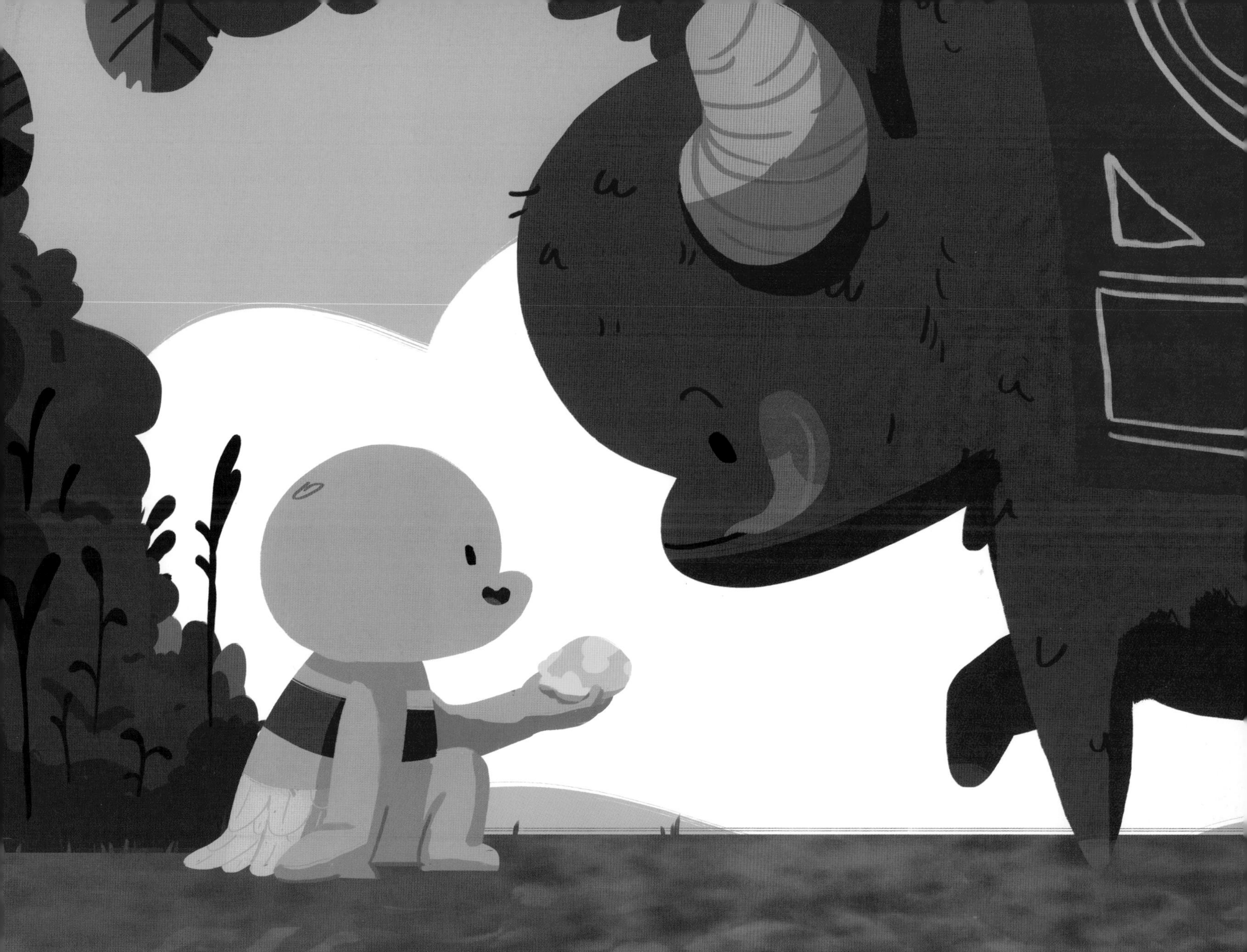

Beast was friendly, Beast was cute.

Beast loved to eat the

VILLAGE FRUIT!

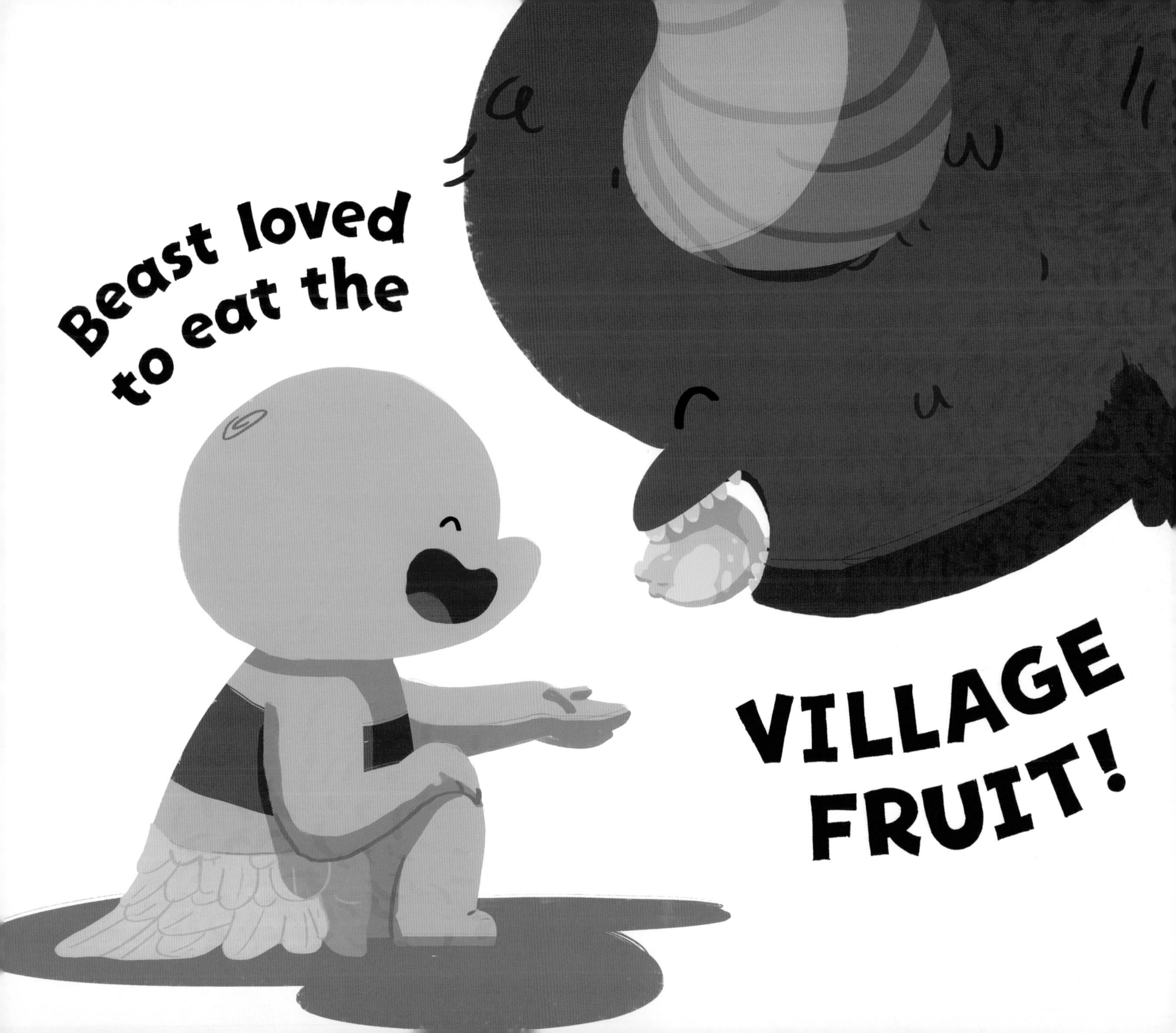

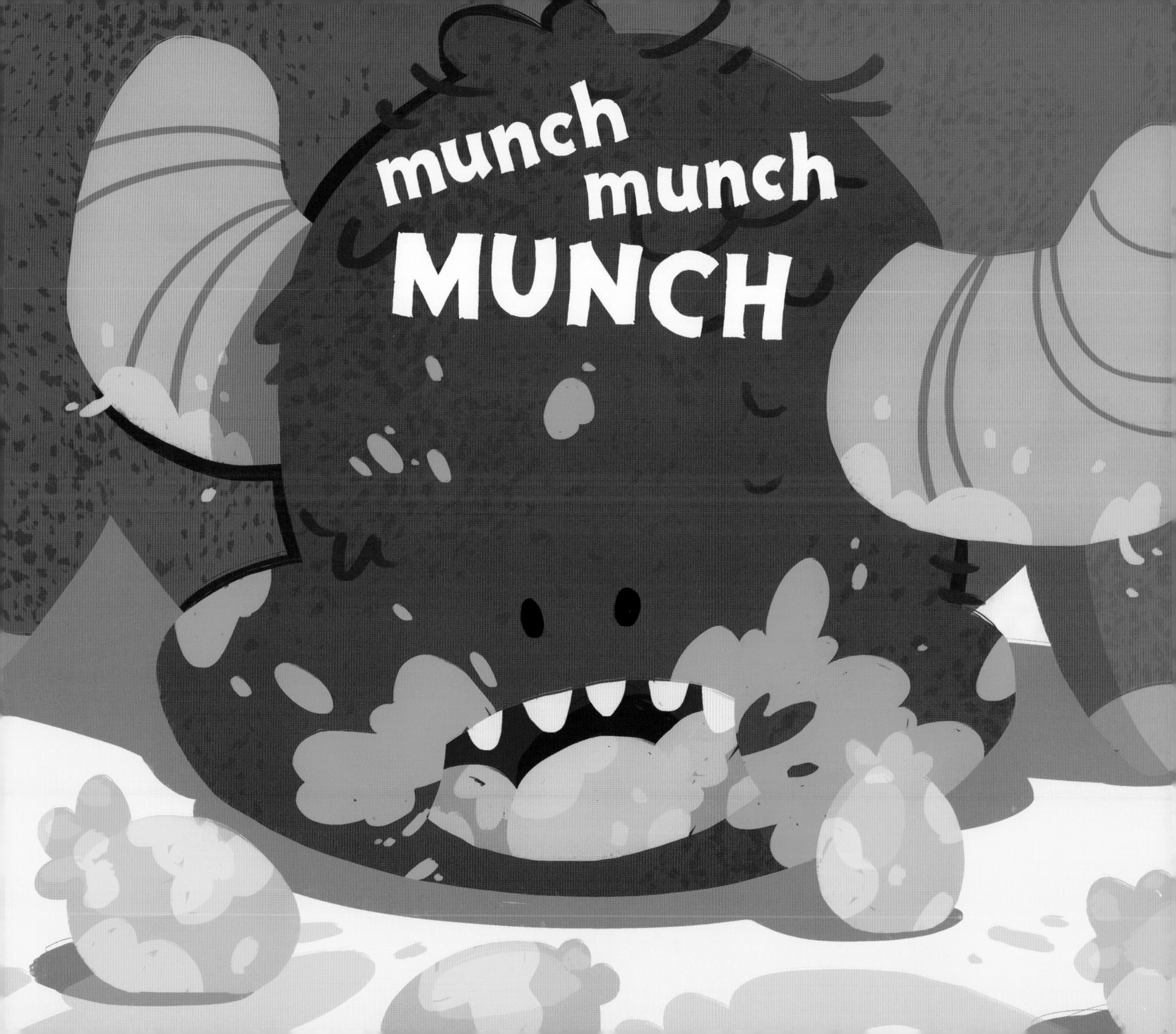

munch
munch
MUNCH

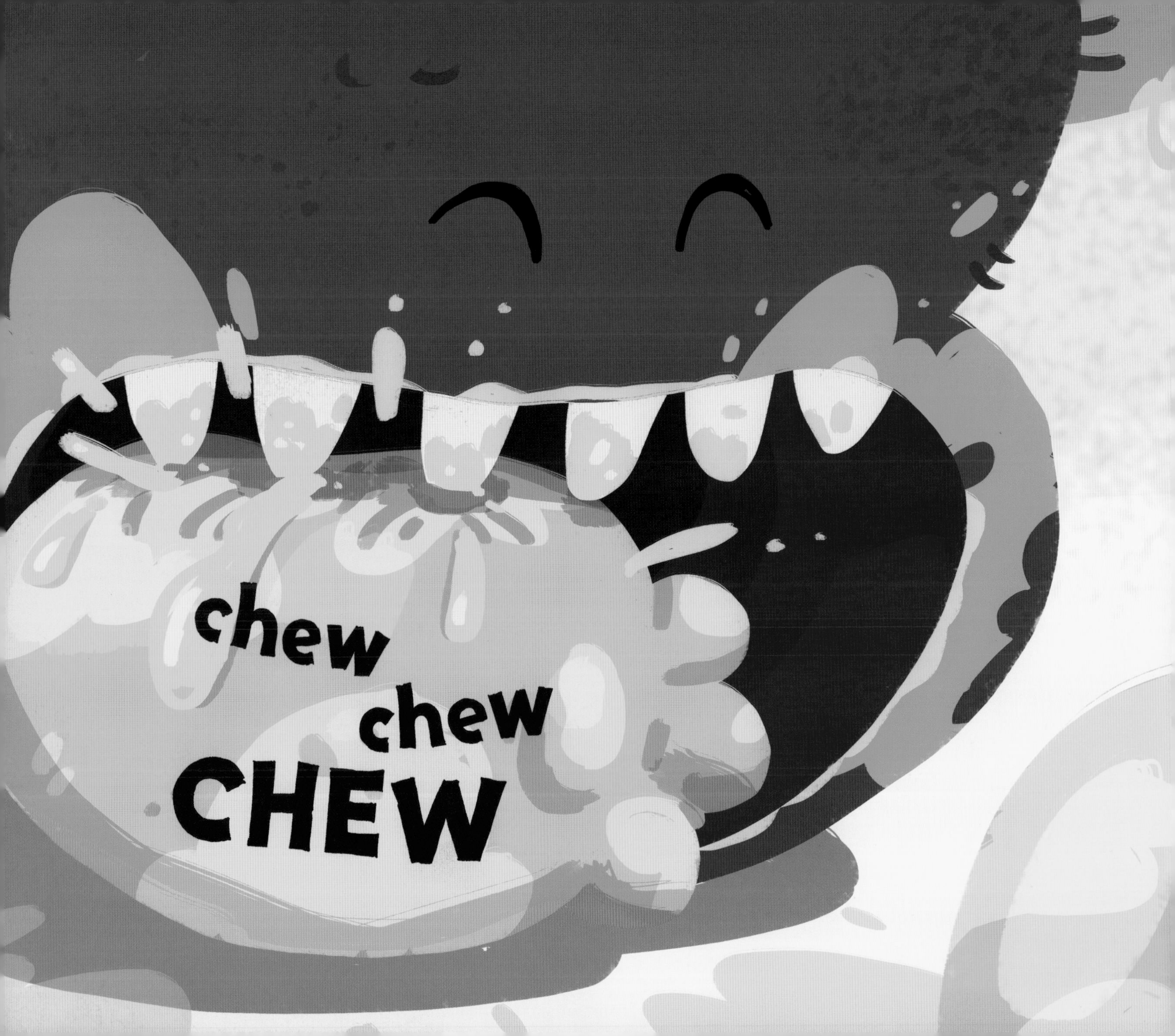
chew
chew
CHEW

Keelee thought of what to do.

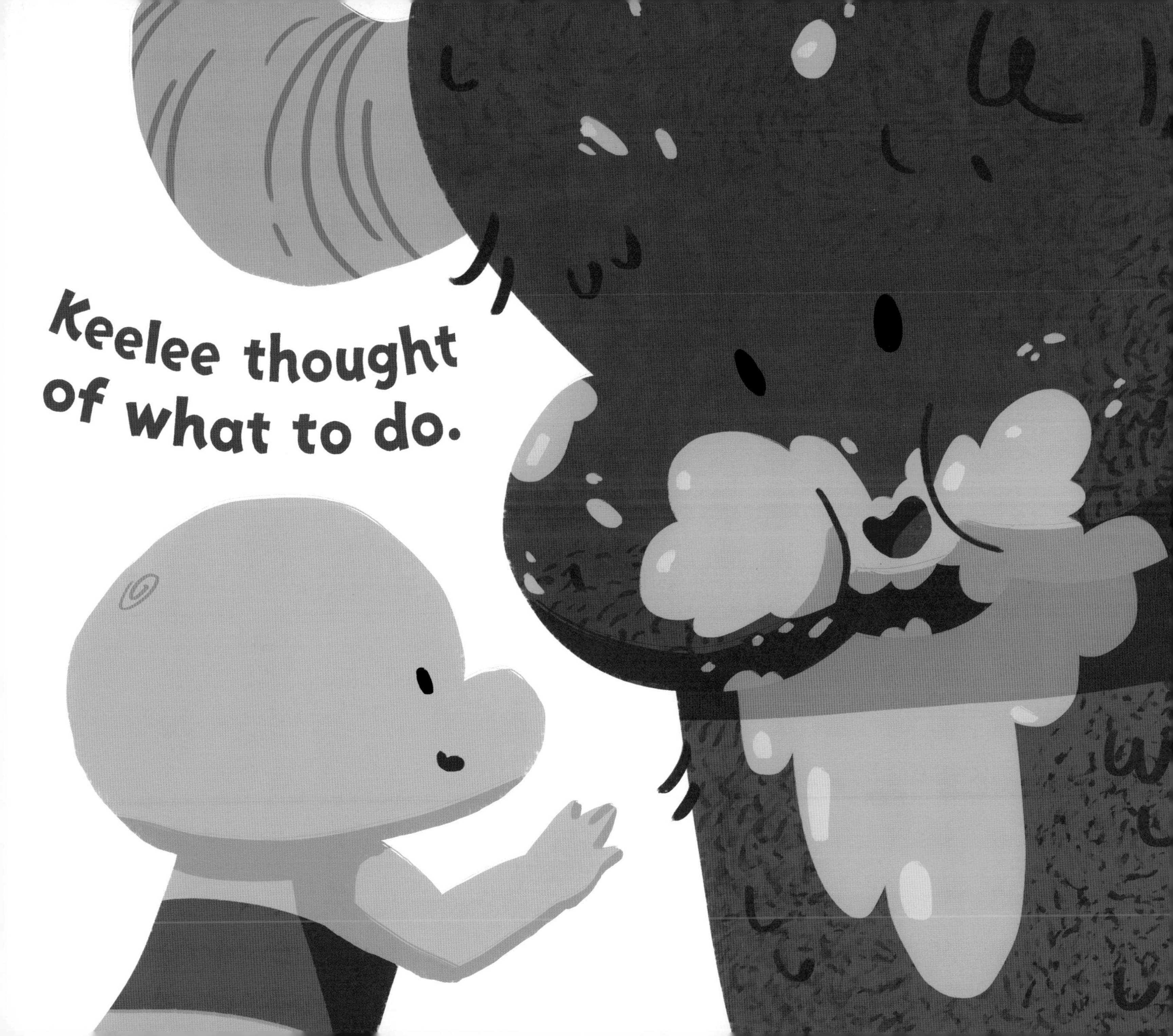

Beast loved to explore and roam,

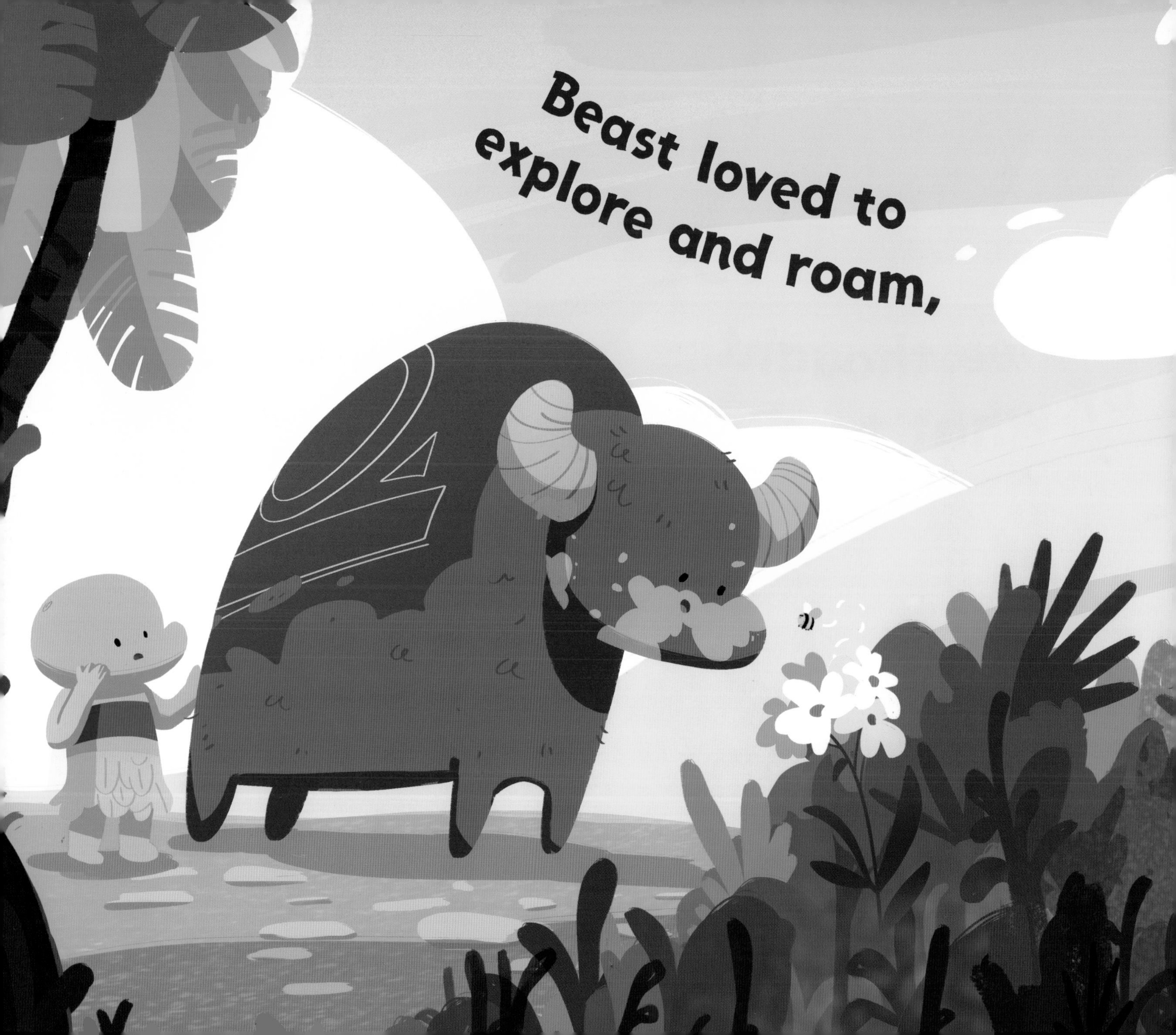

but he was lost and far from home.

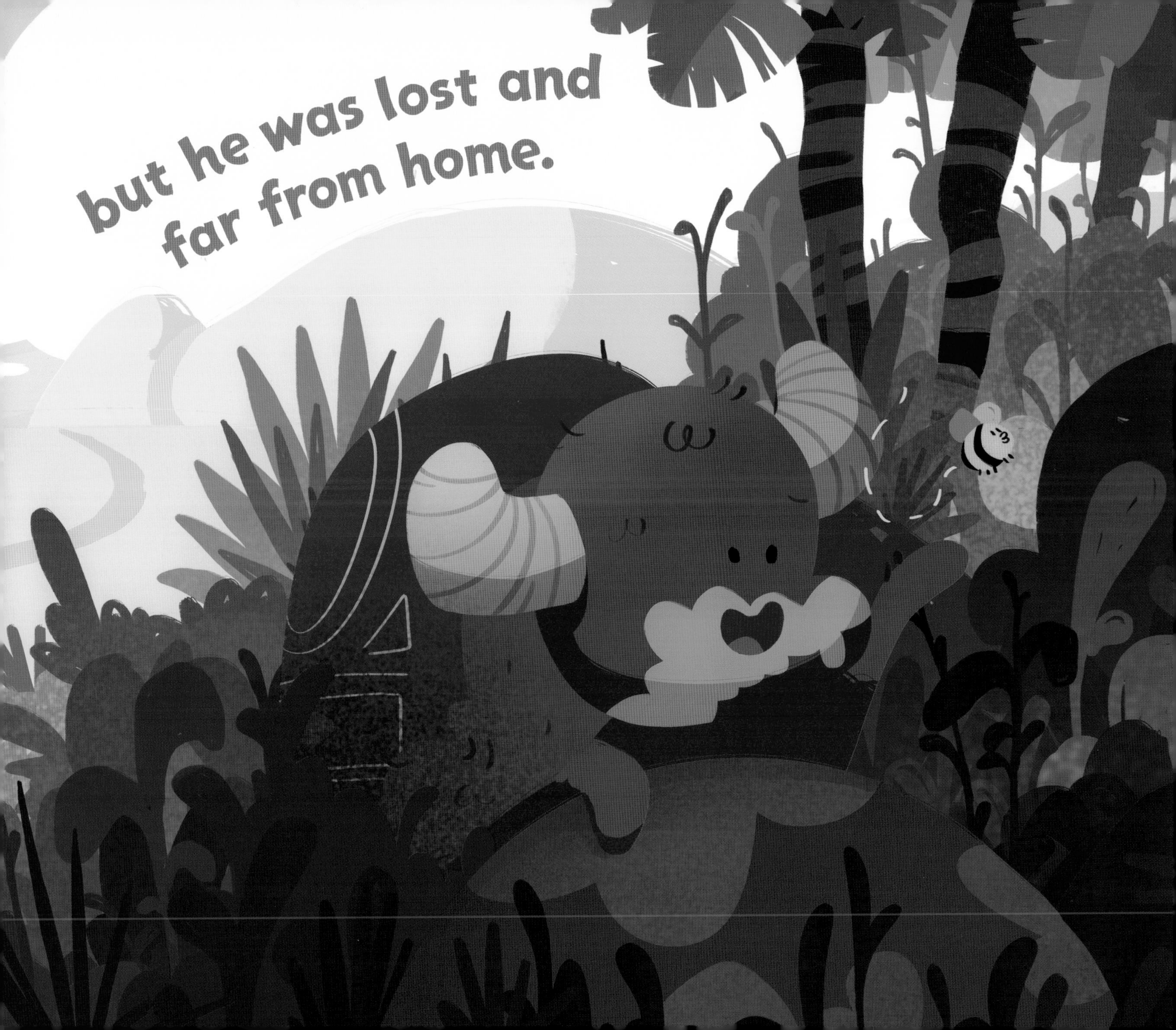

Keelee's village in the west
was where the sun came down to rest.

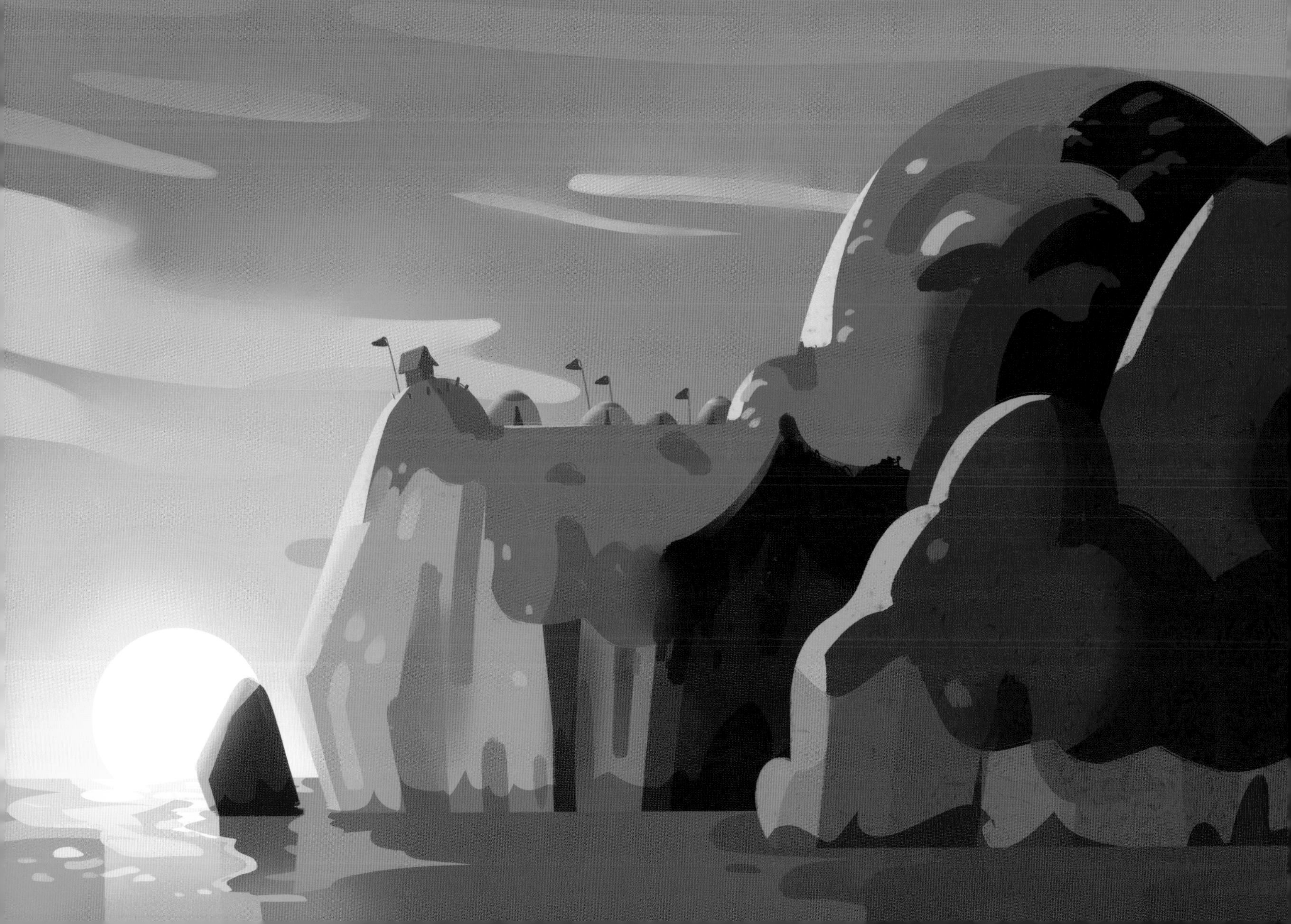

Beast lived where the sun would rise,
lighting up the island skies.

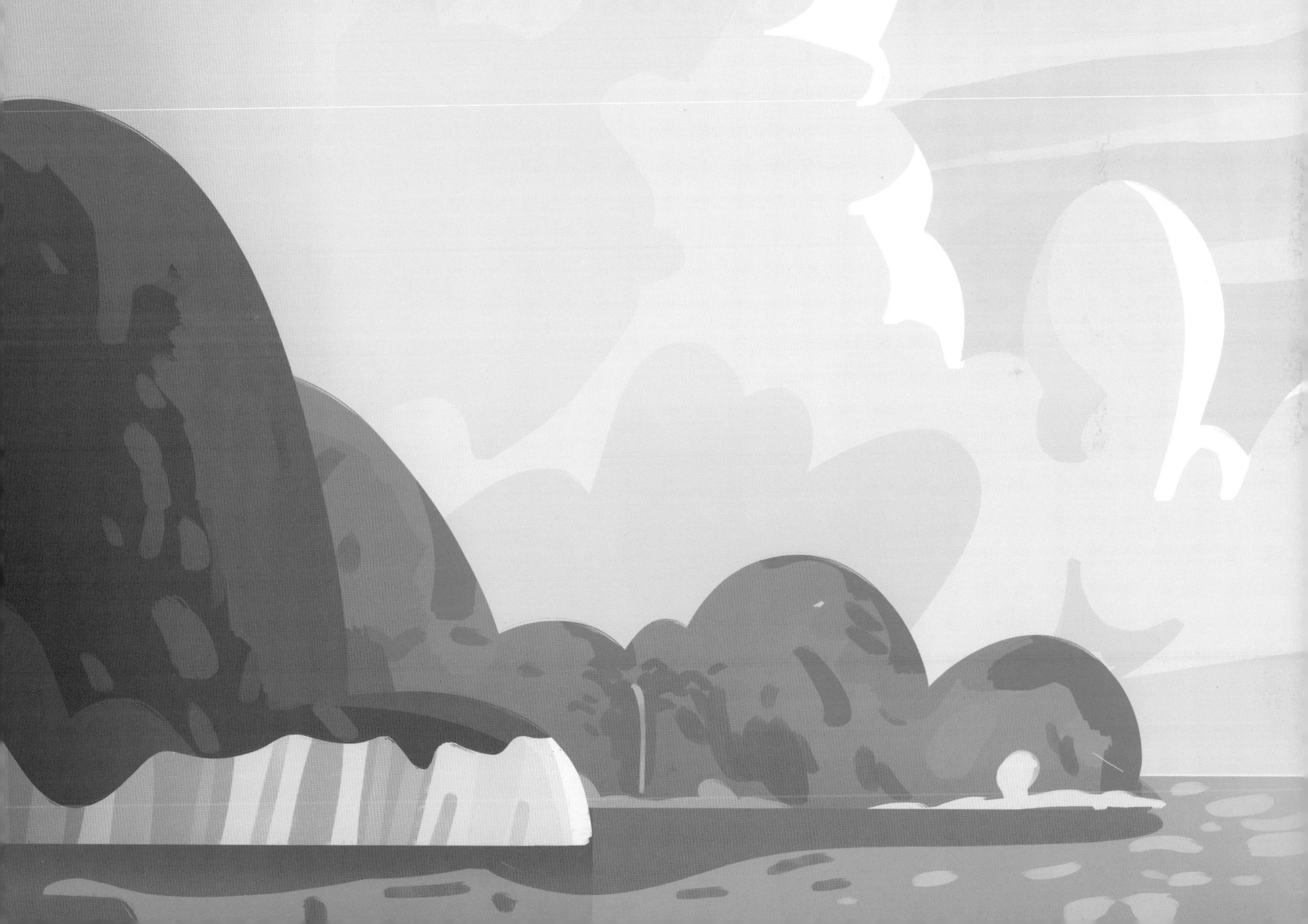

So little Keelee led the beast.
Together they both headed east!

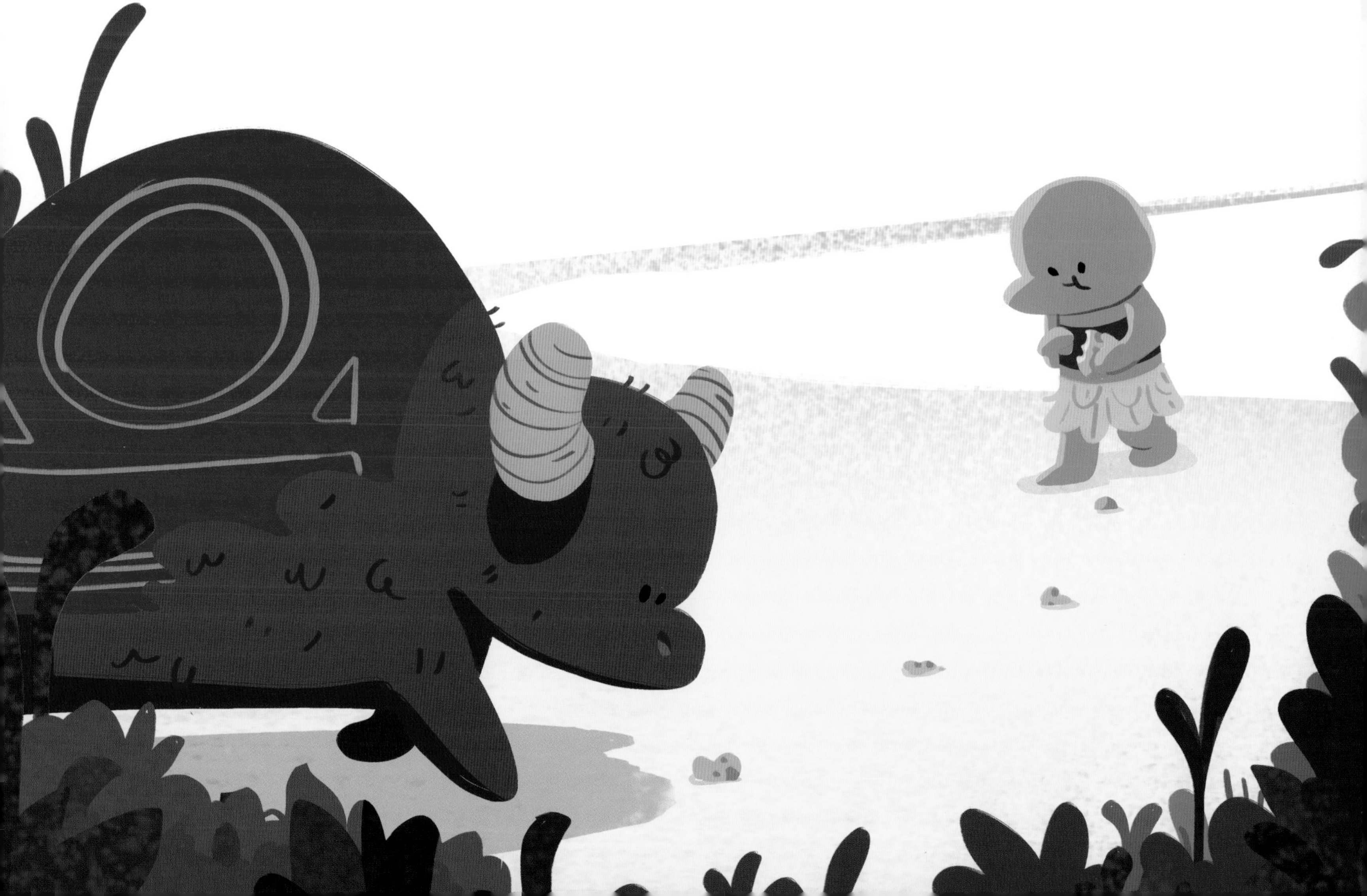

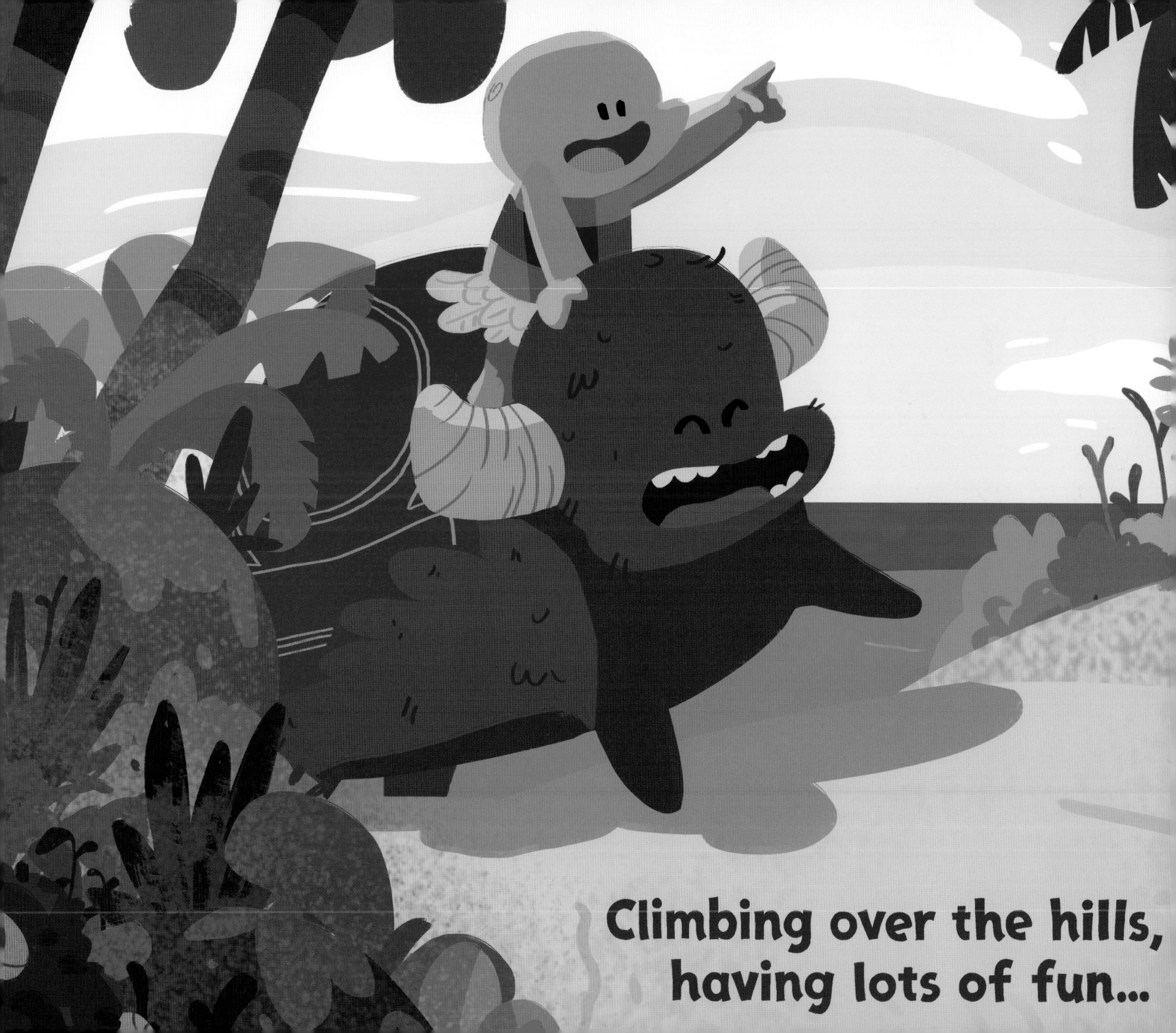

Climbing over the hills,
having lots of fun...

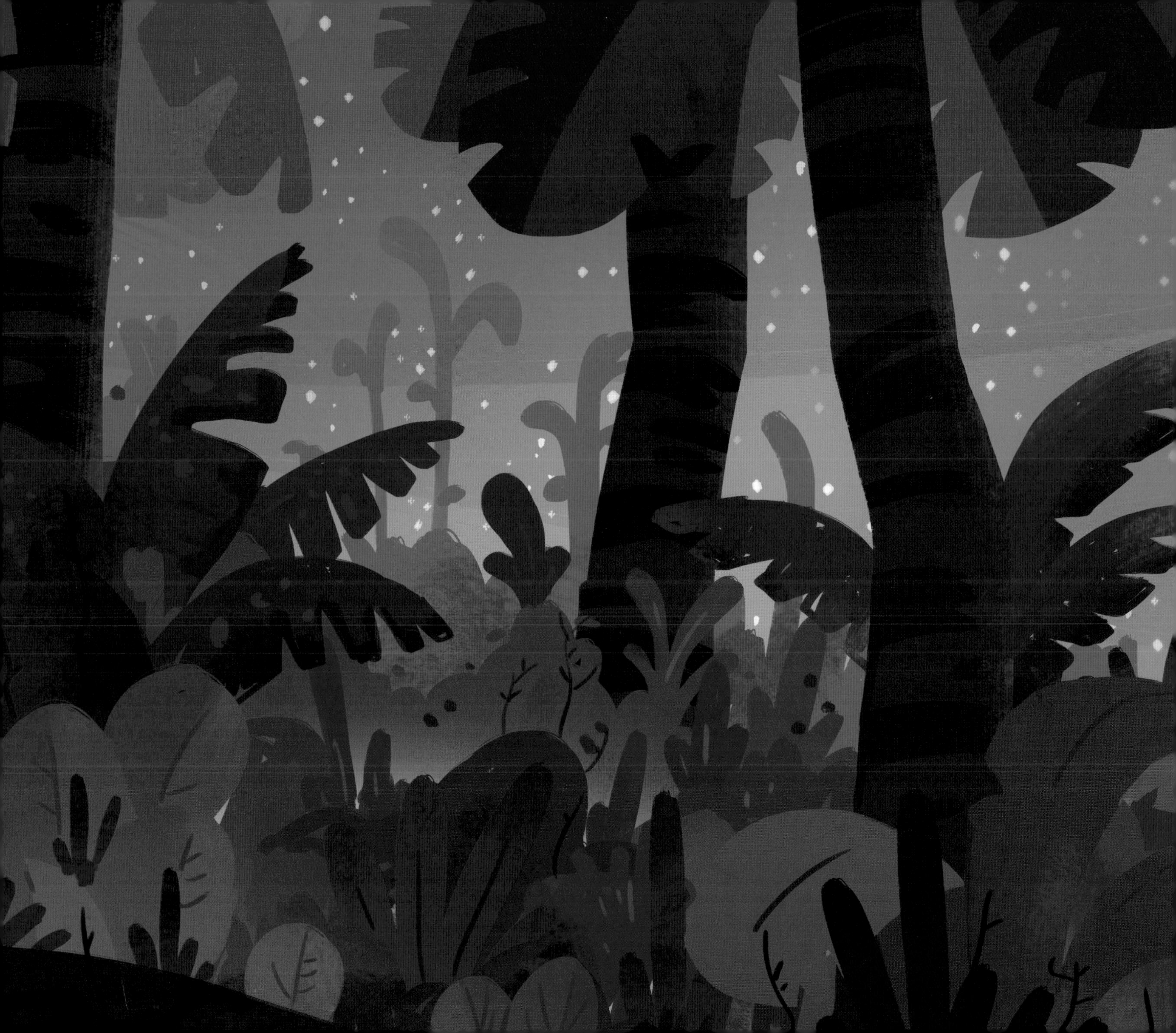

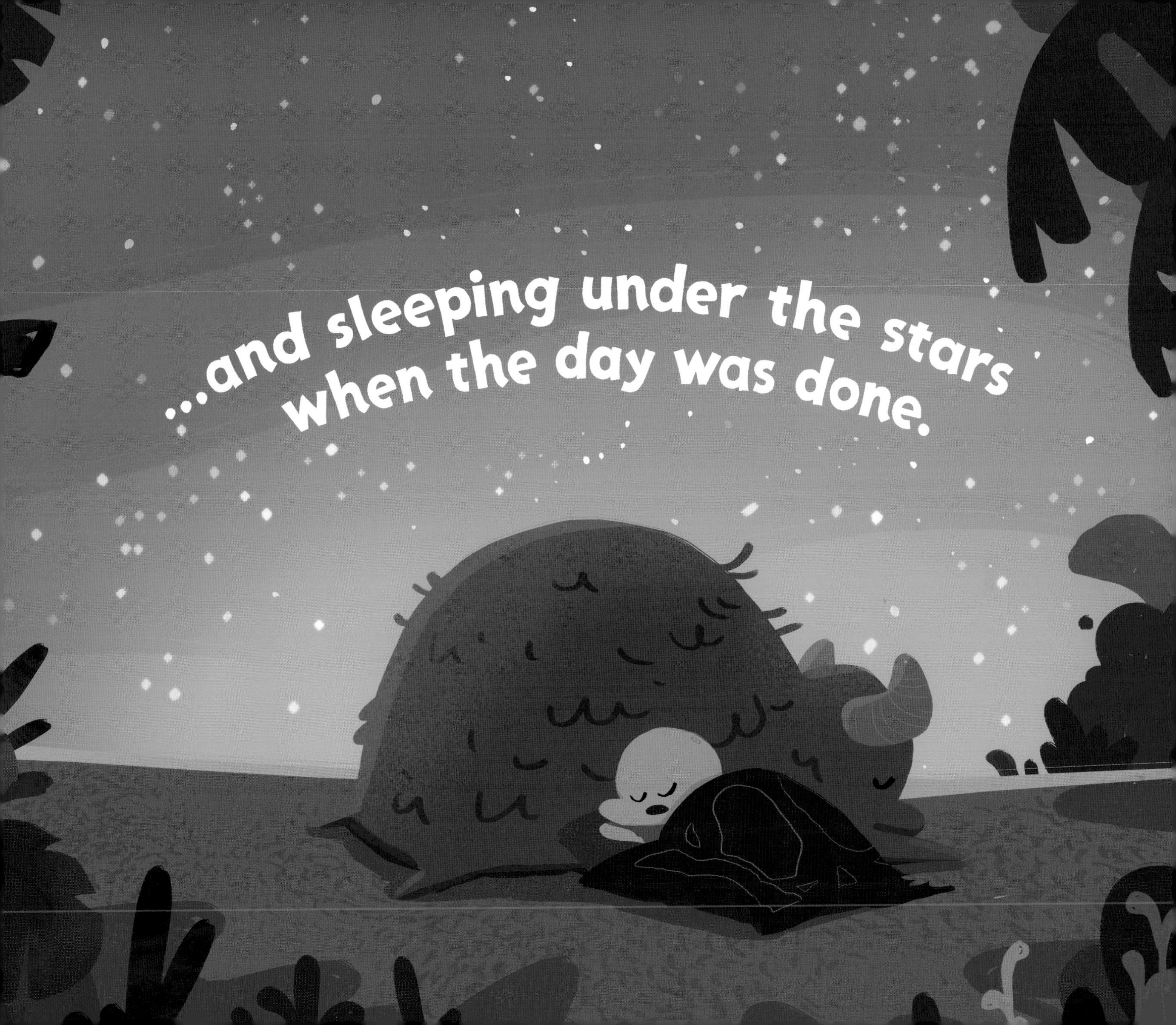

...and sleeping under the stars
when the day was done.

Keelee sang
her favorite song...

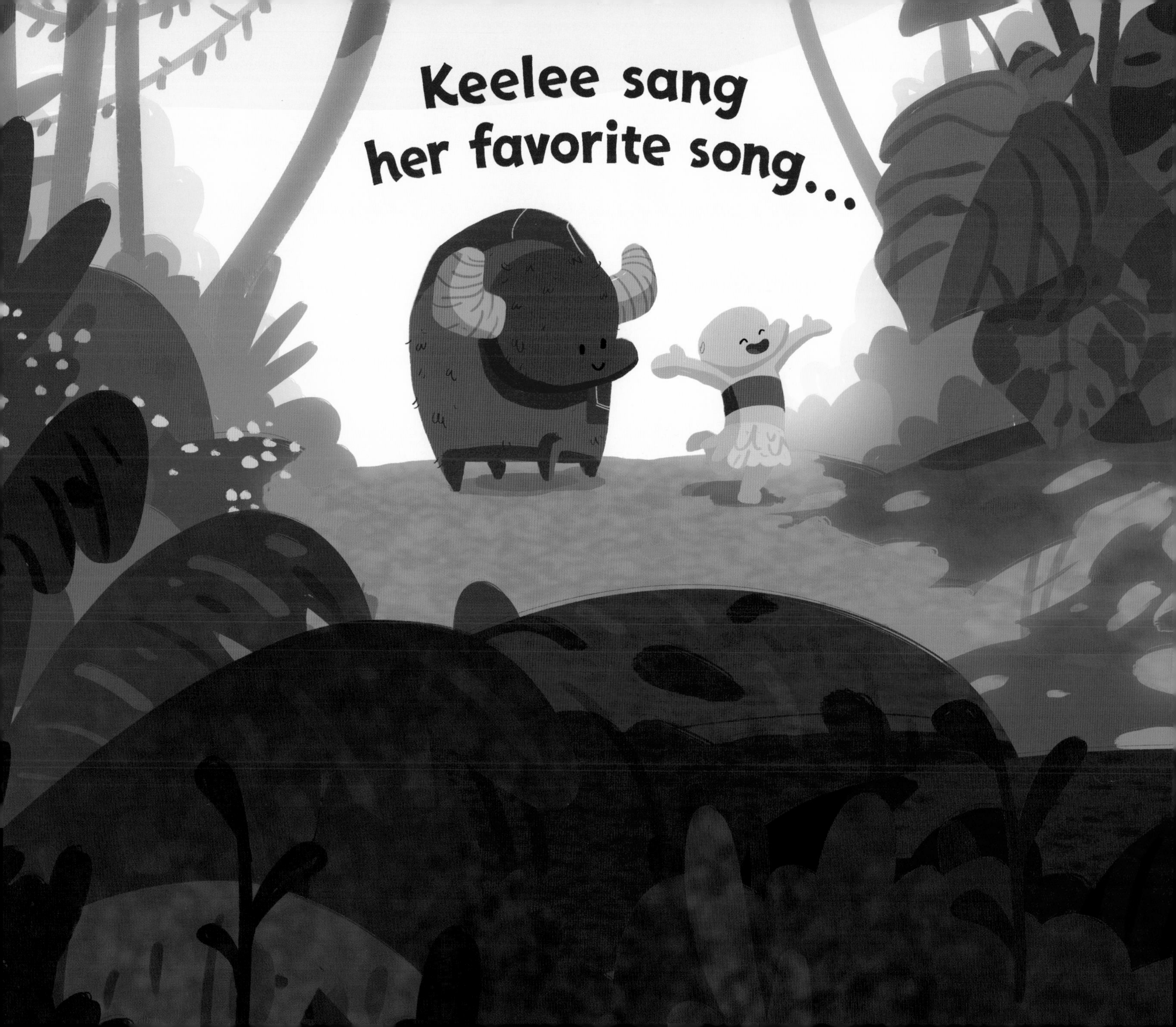

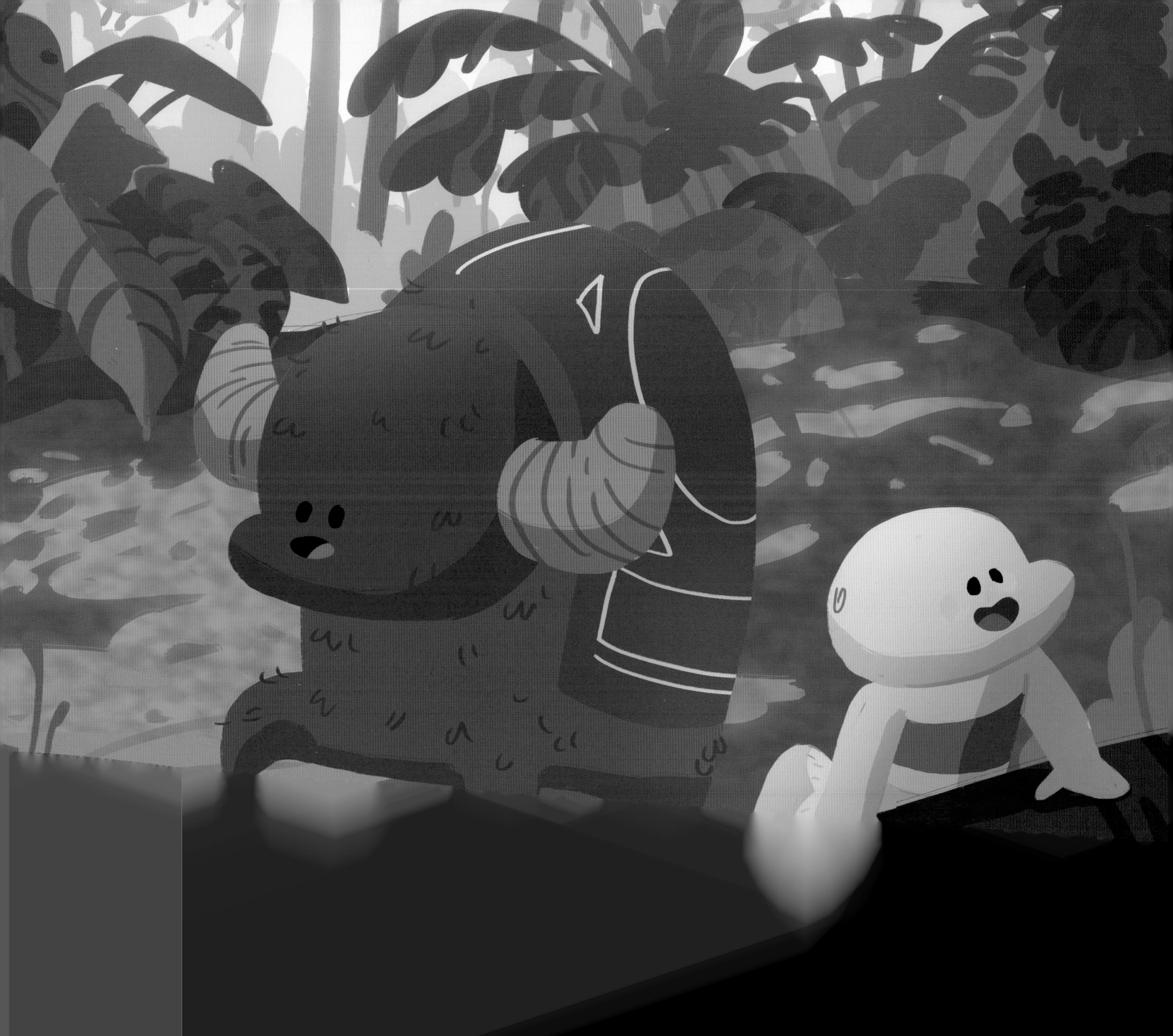

Up

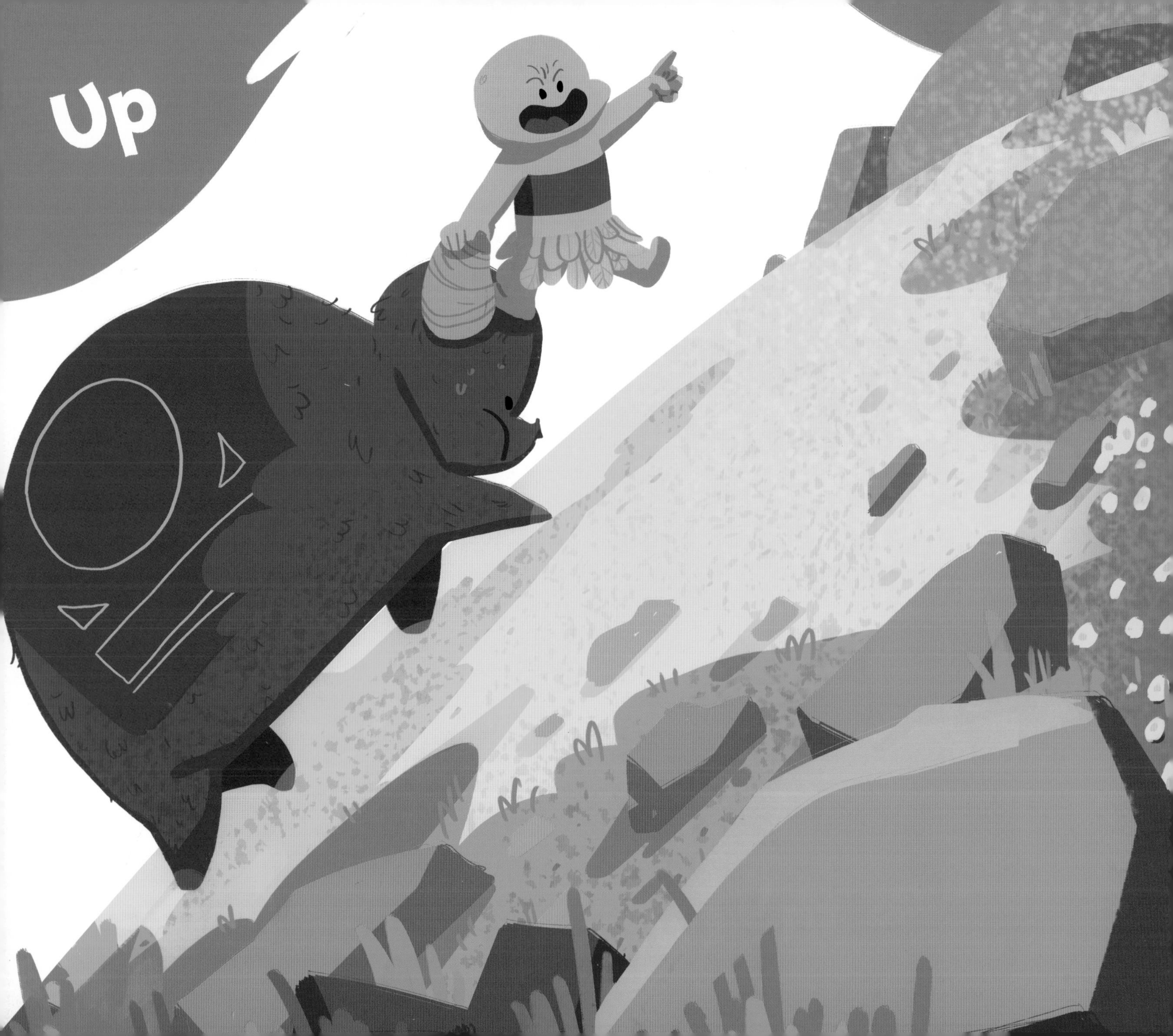

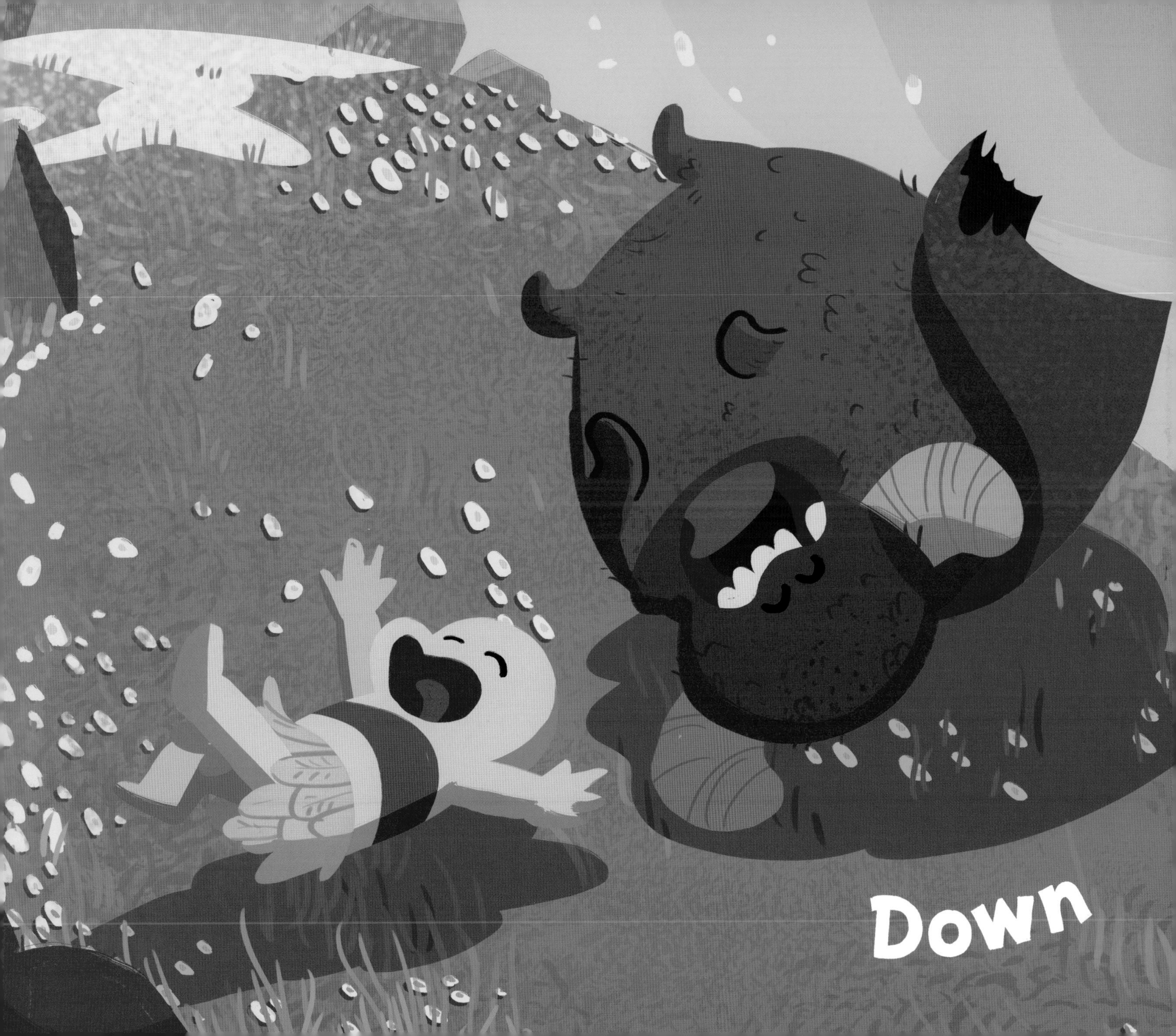

Down

Left

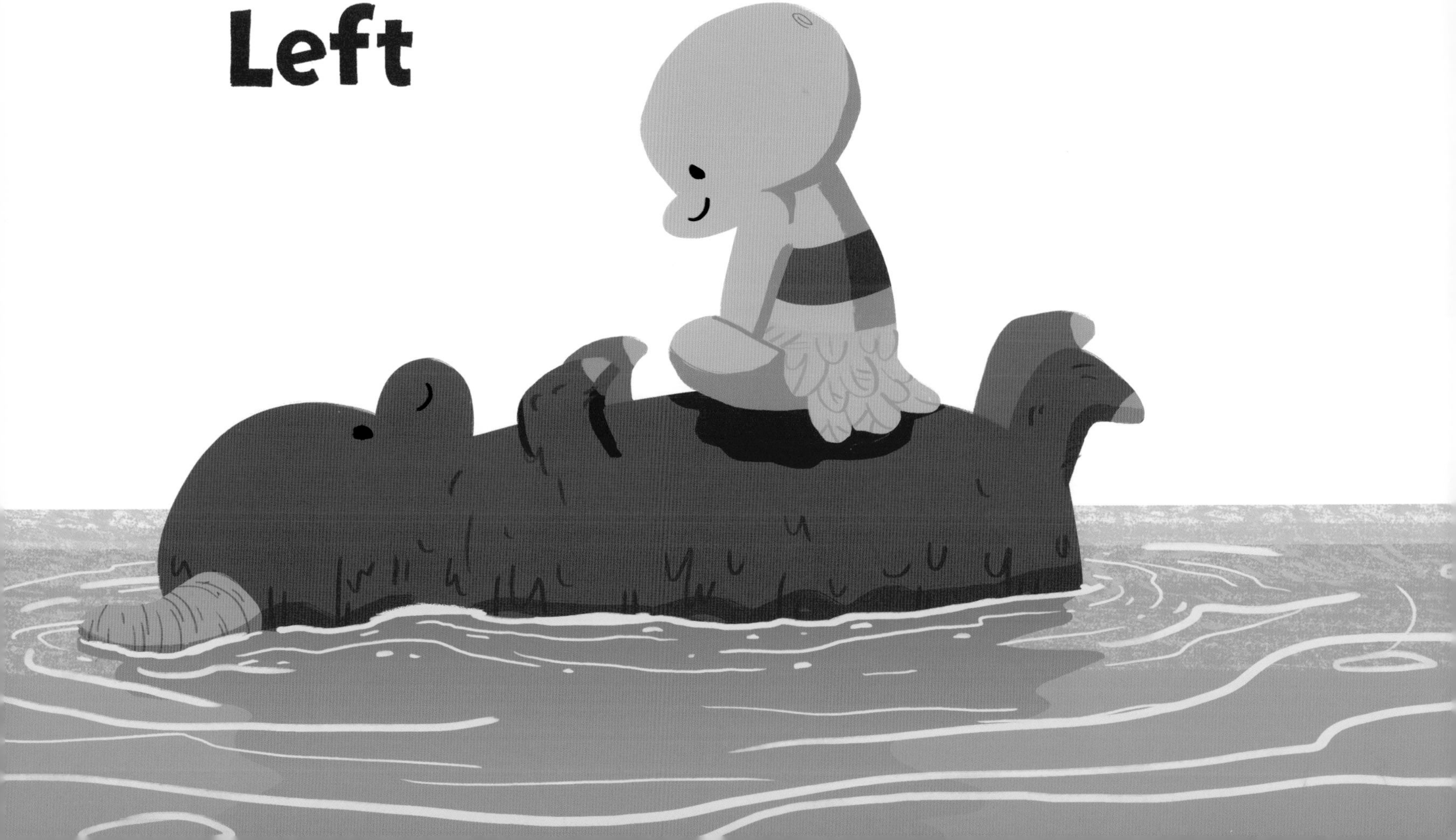

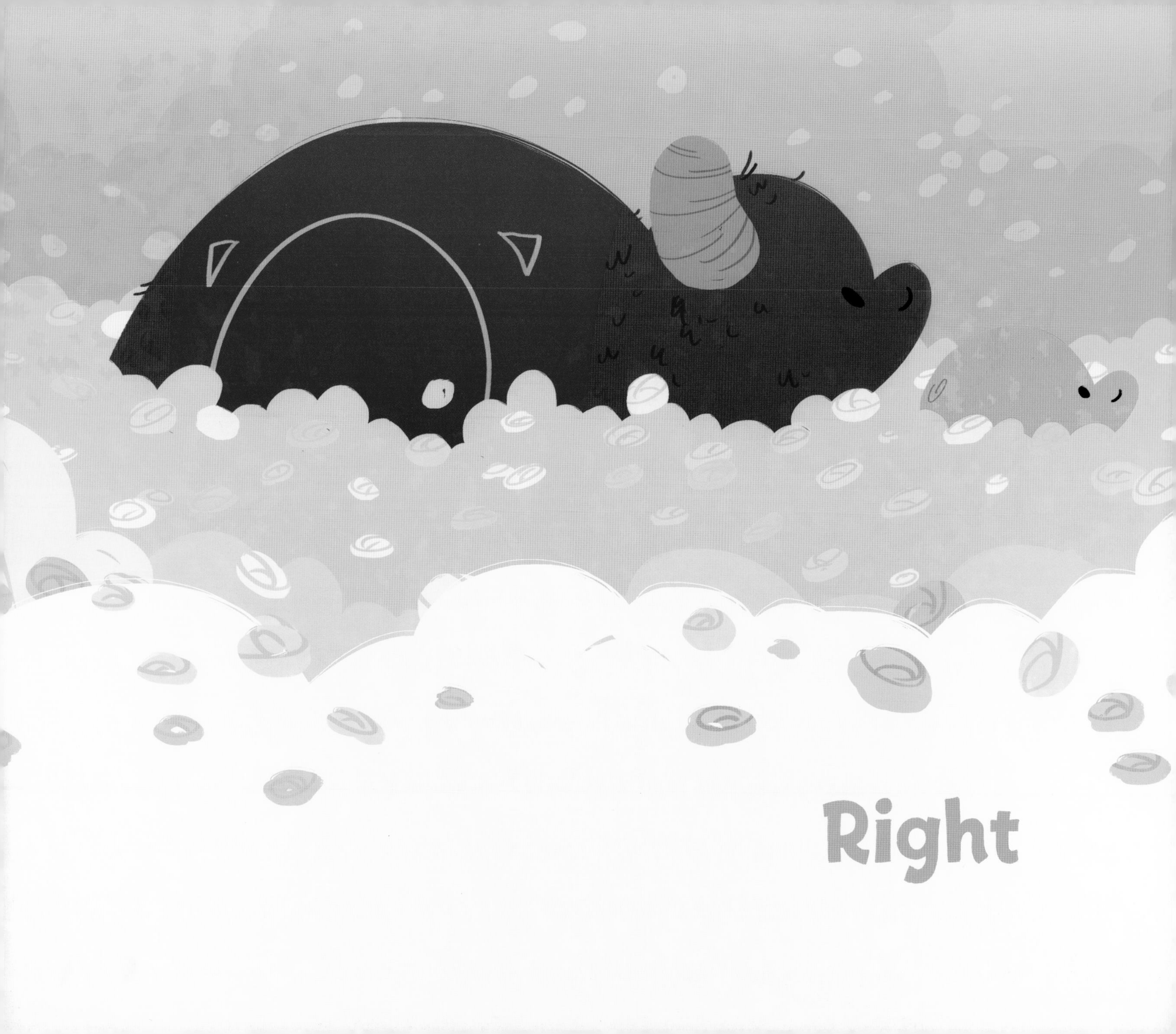

Right

Morning

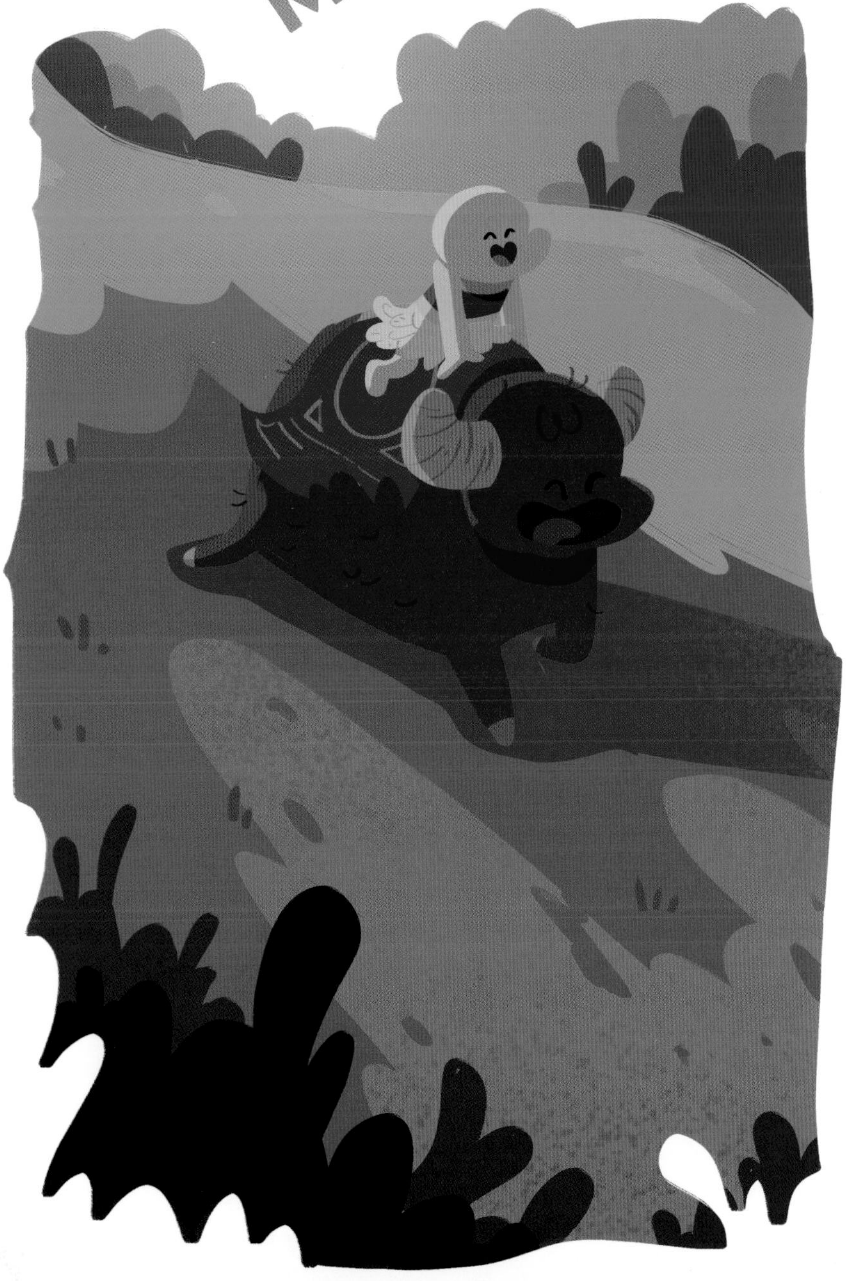

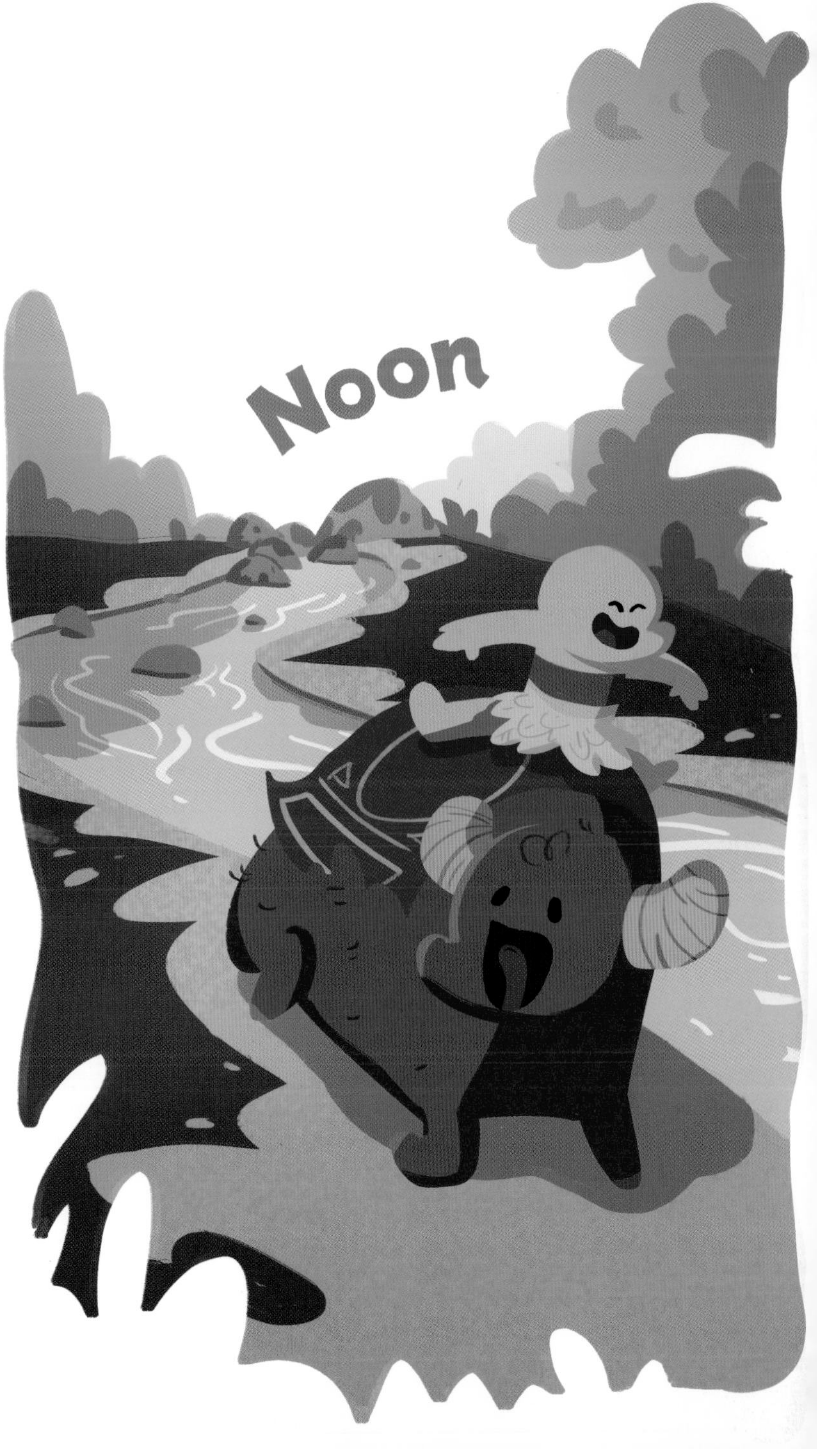
Noon

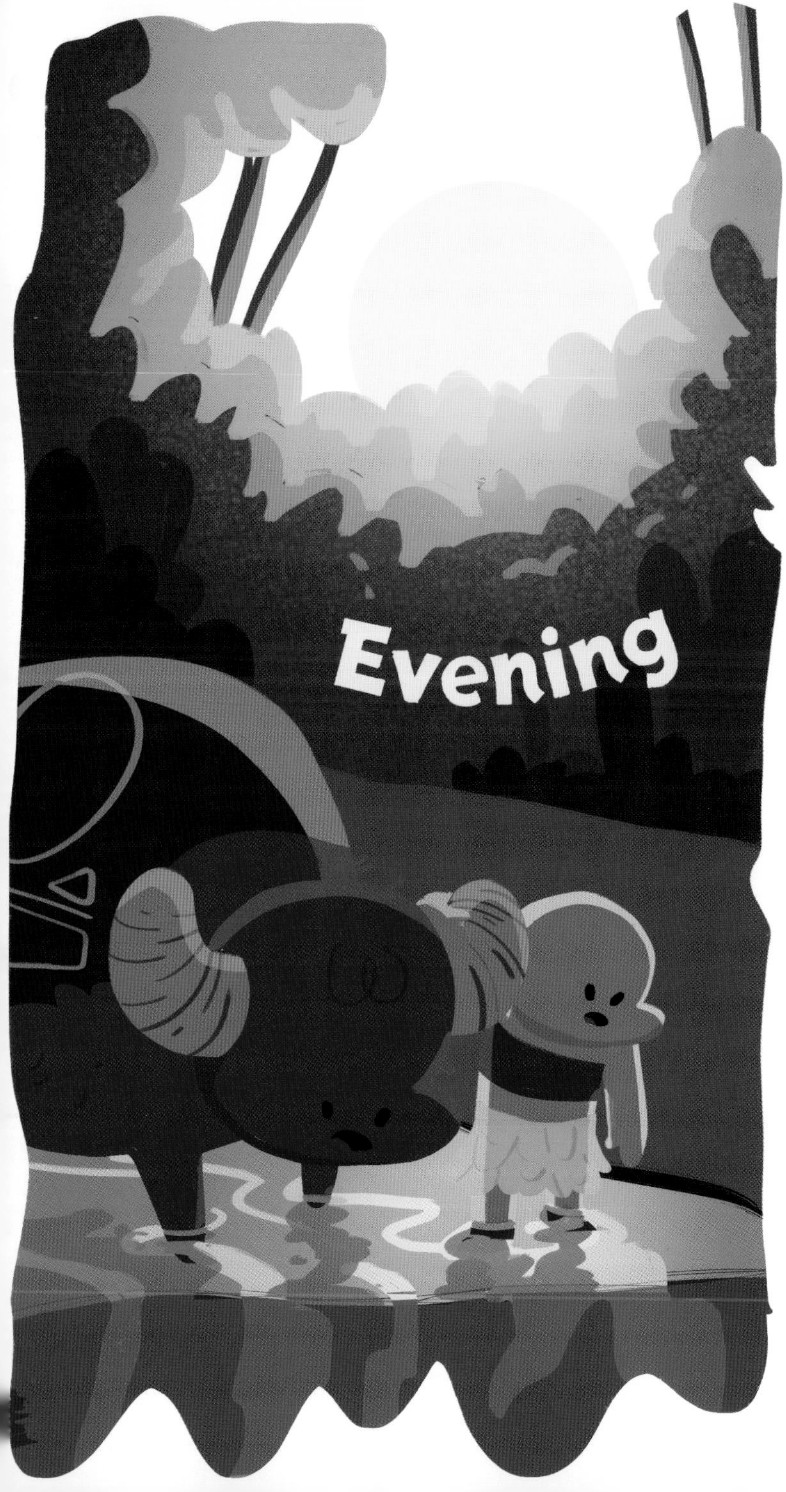
Evening

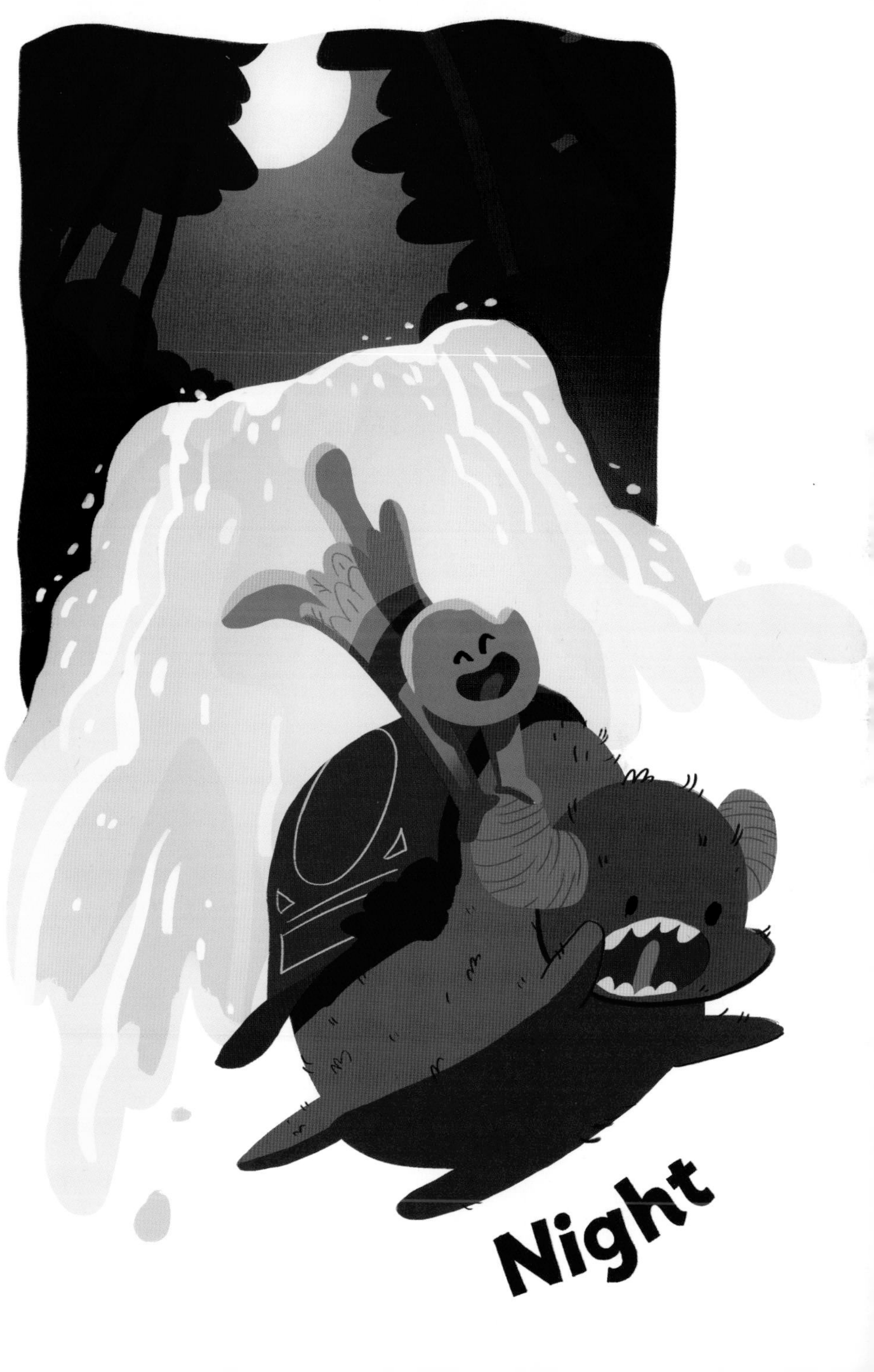
Night

Suddenly, there was a great surprise...

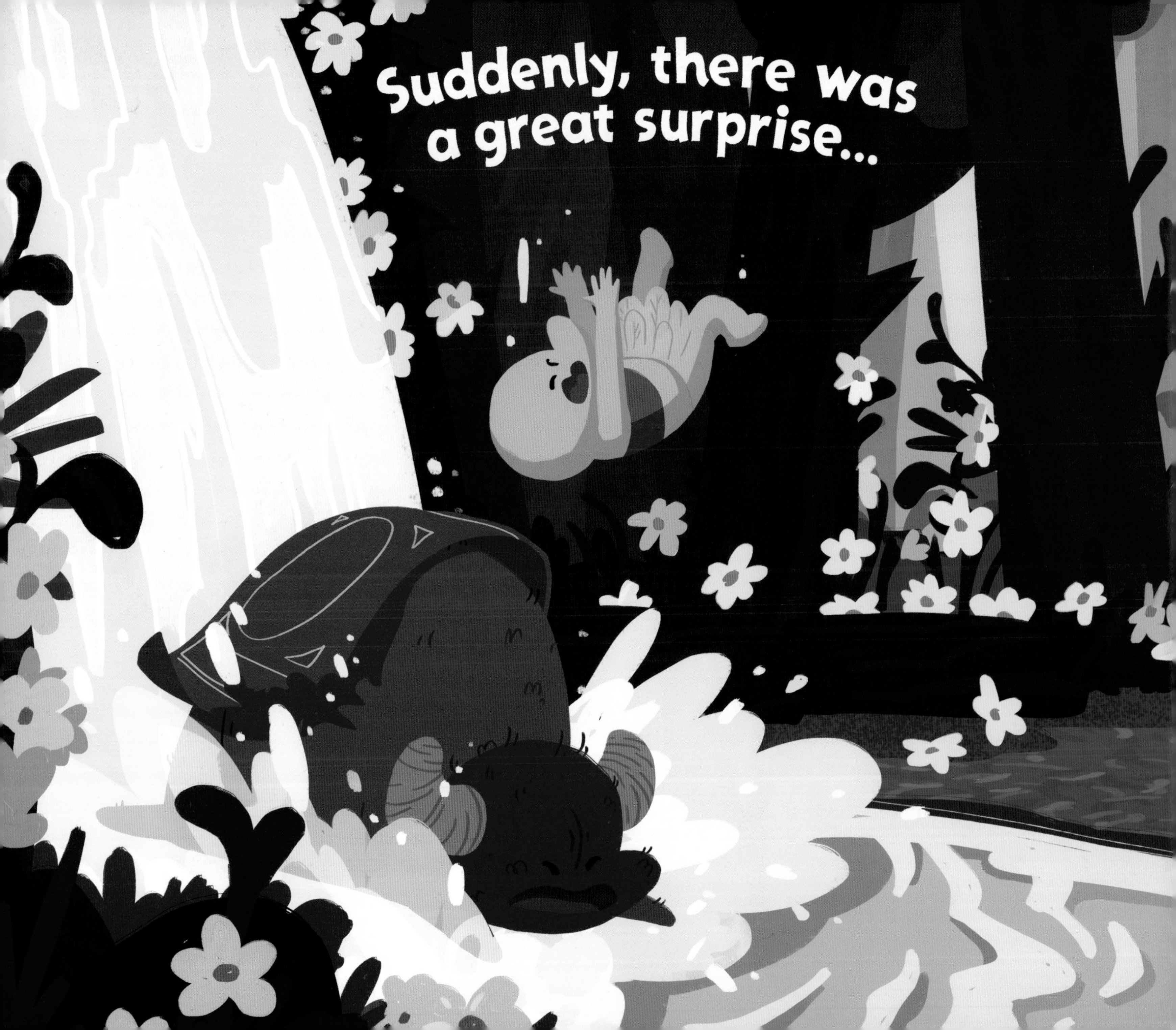

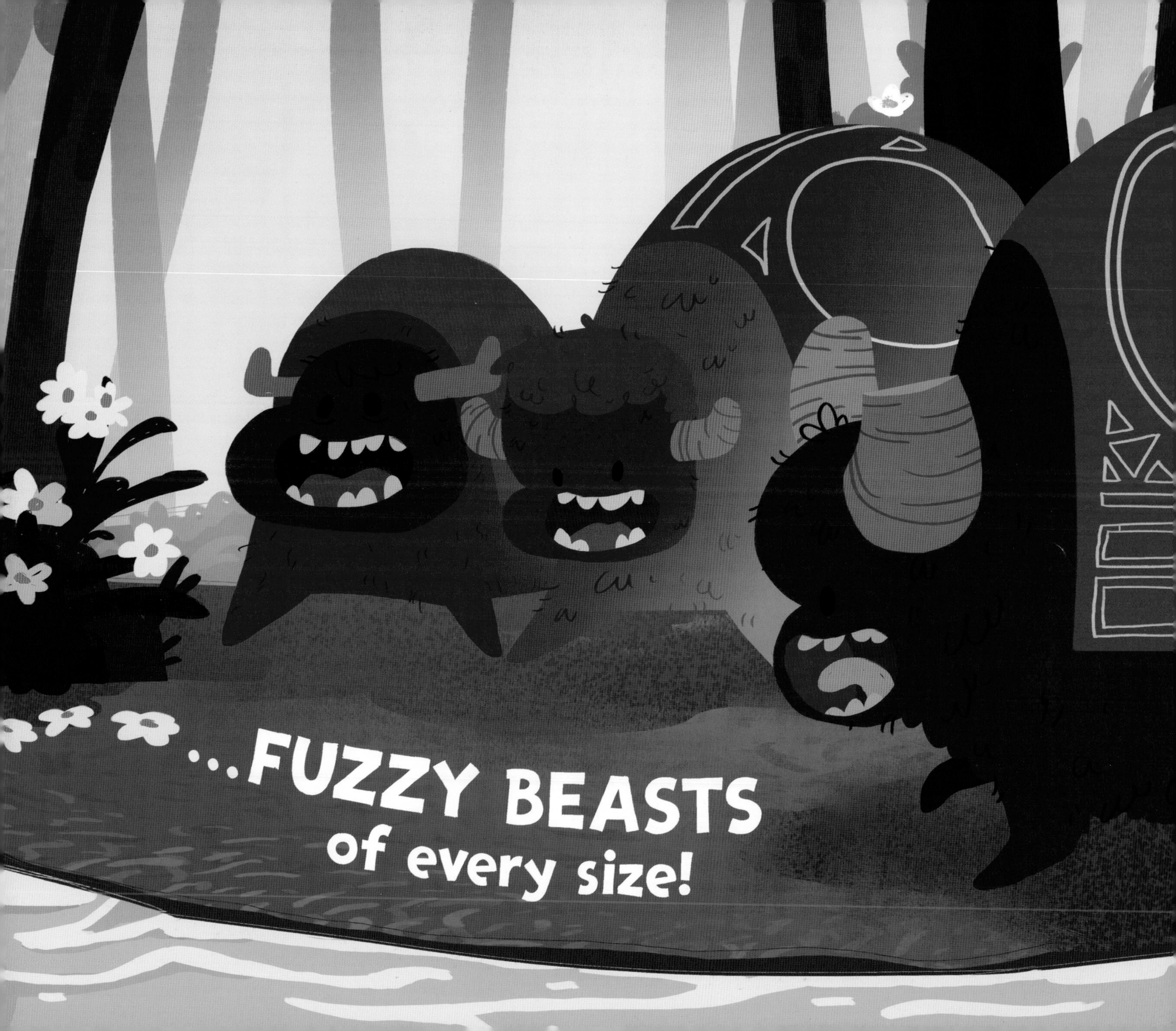

...FUZZY BEASTS of every size!

Beast had his own village too,

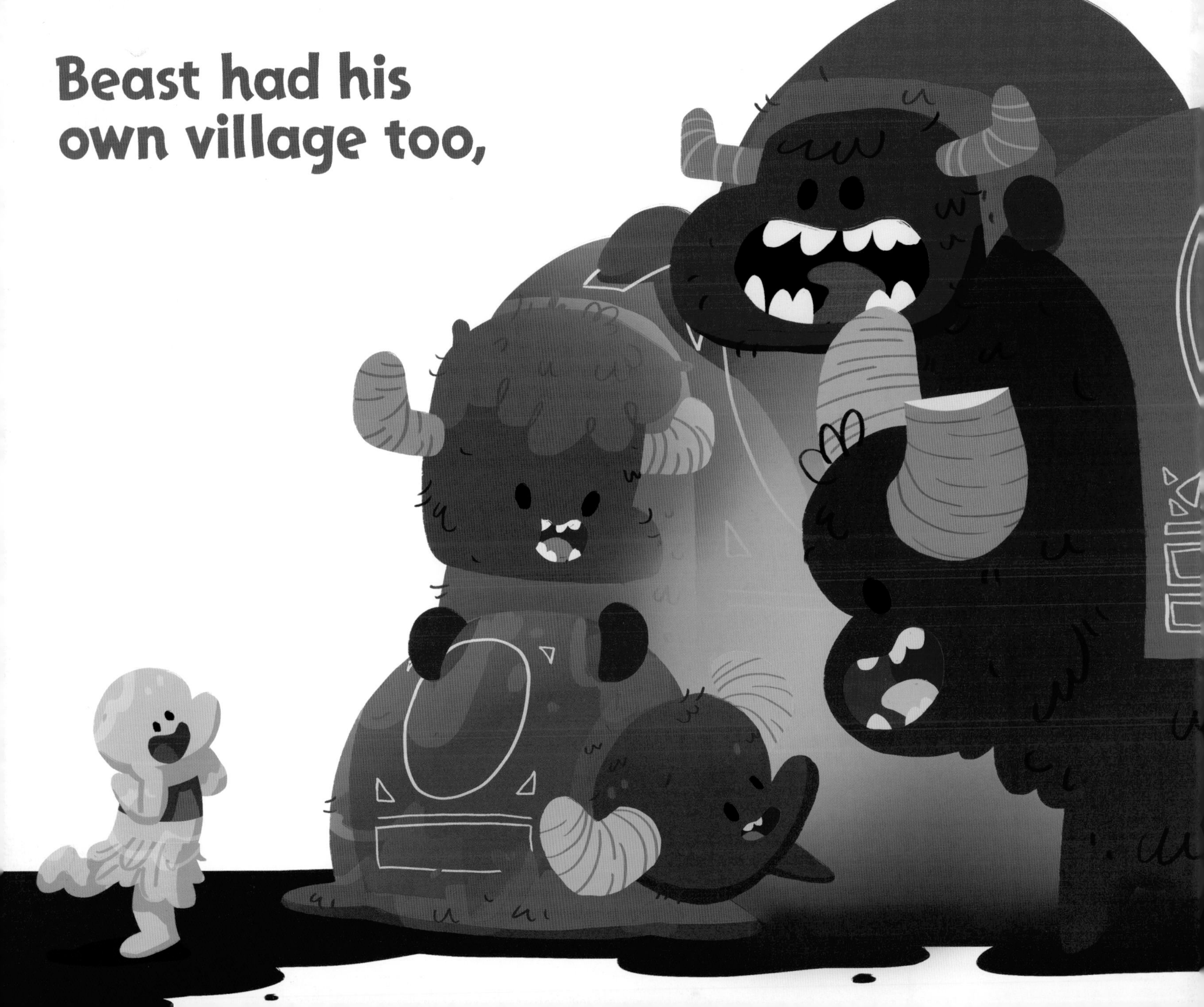

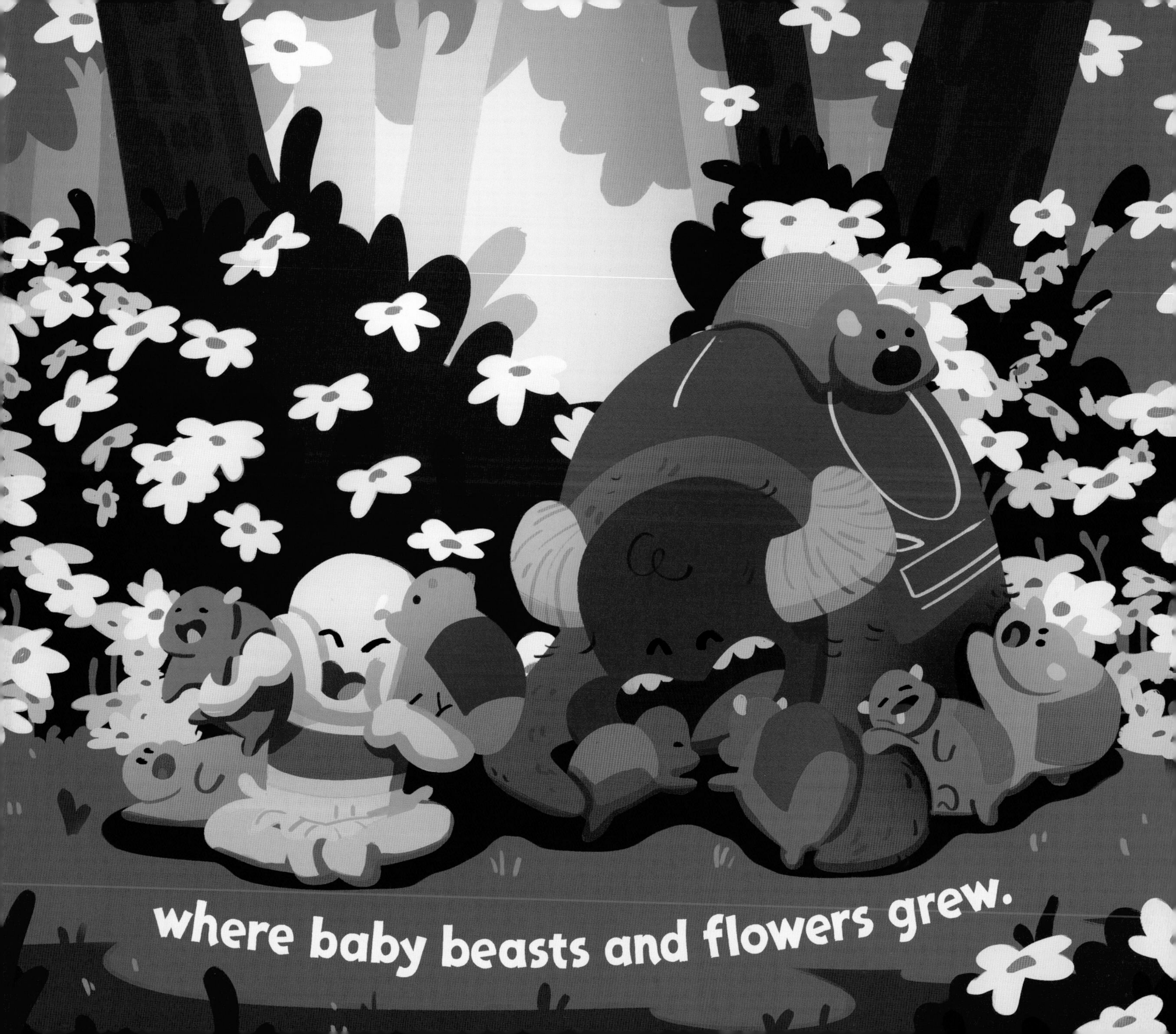

where baby beasts and flowers grew.

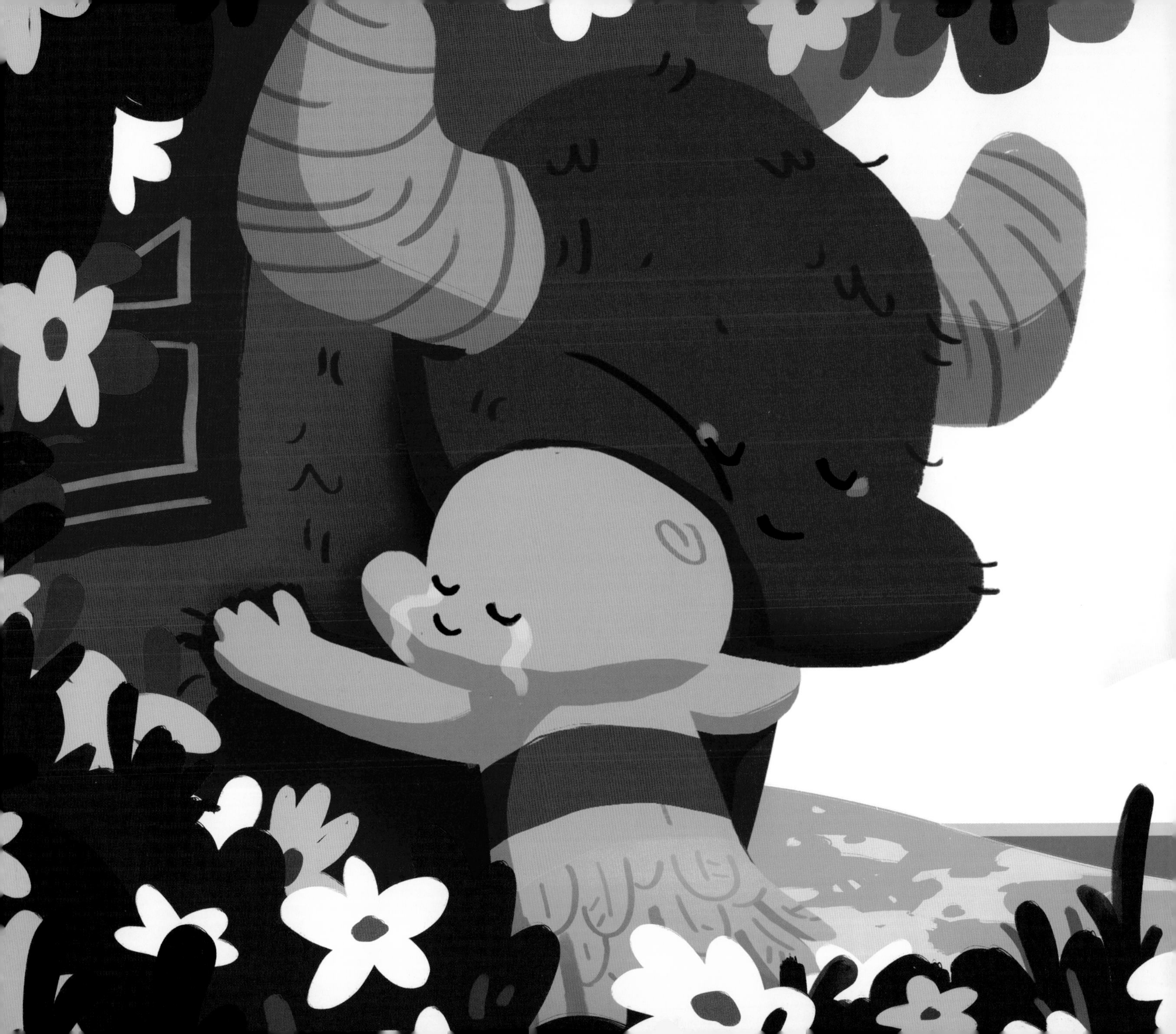

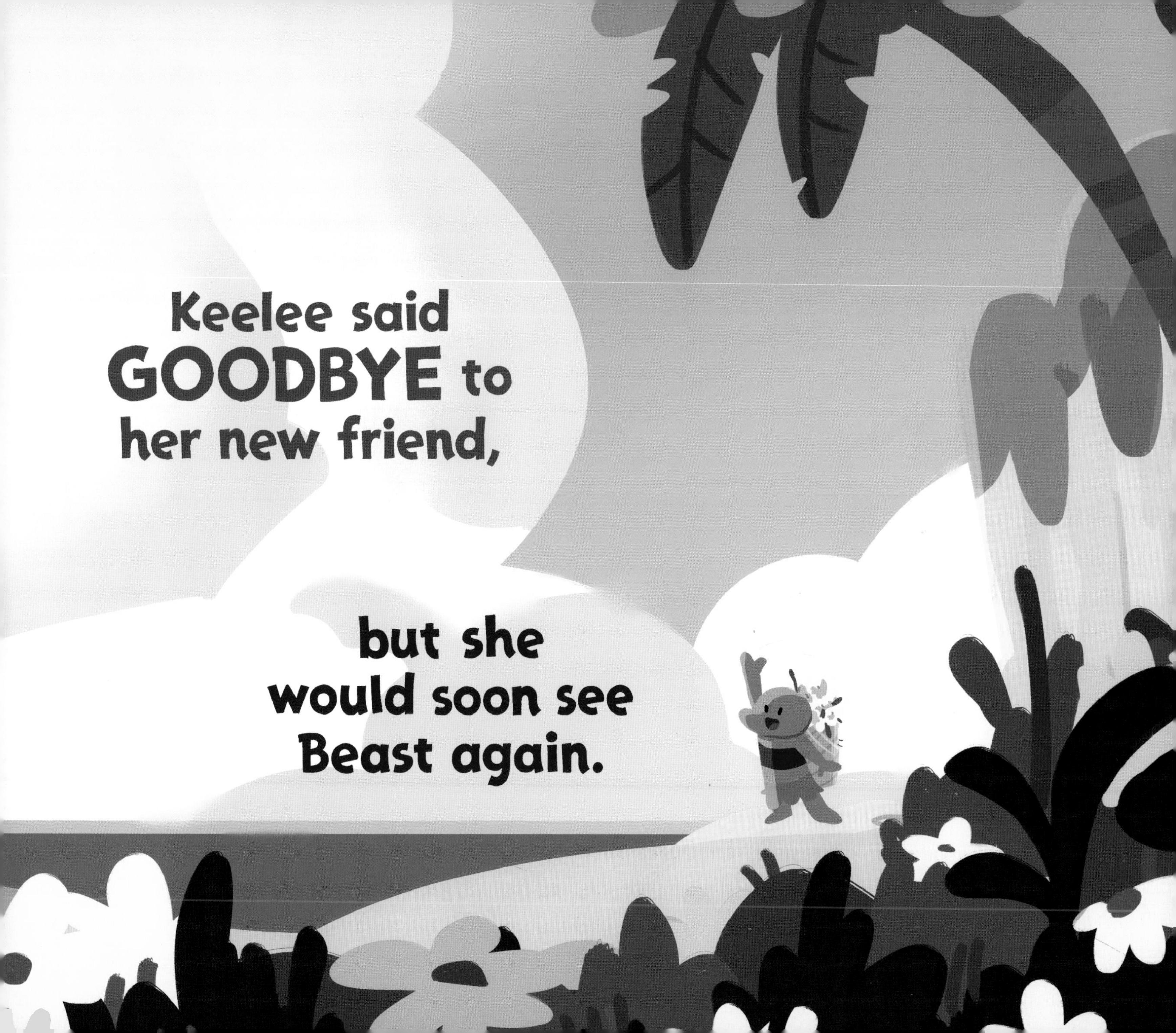

Keelee said **GOODBYE** to her new friend,

but she would soon see Beast again.

Beast lived not too far away.

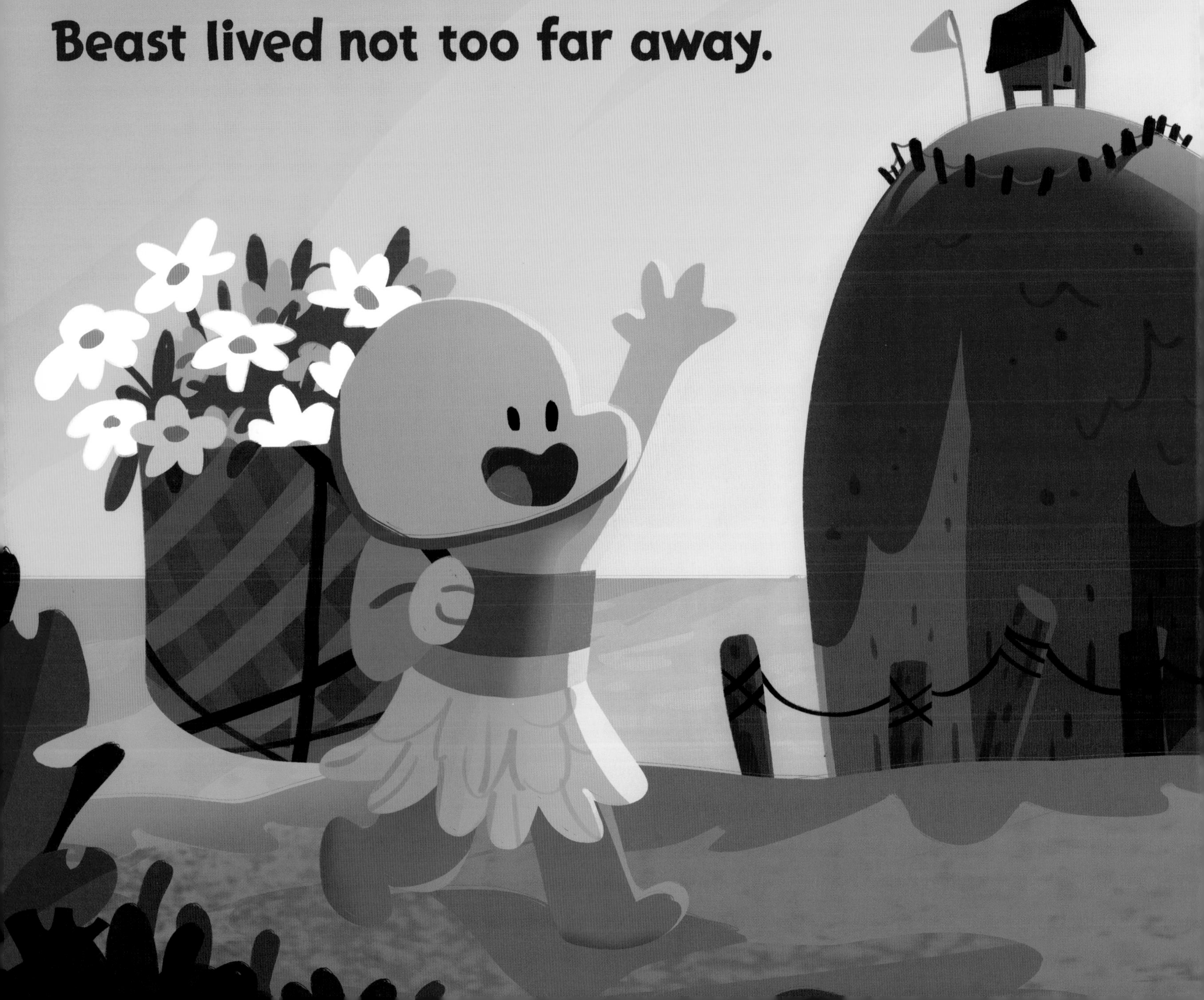

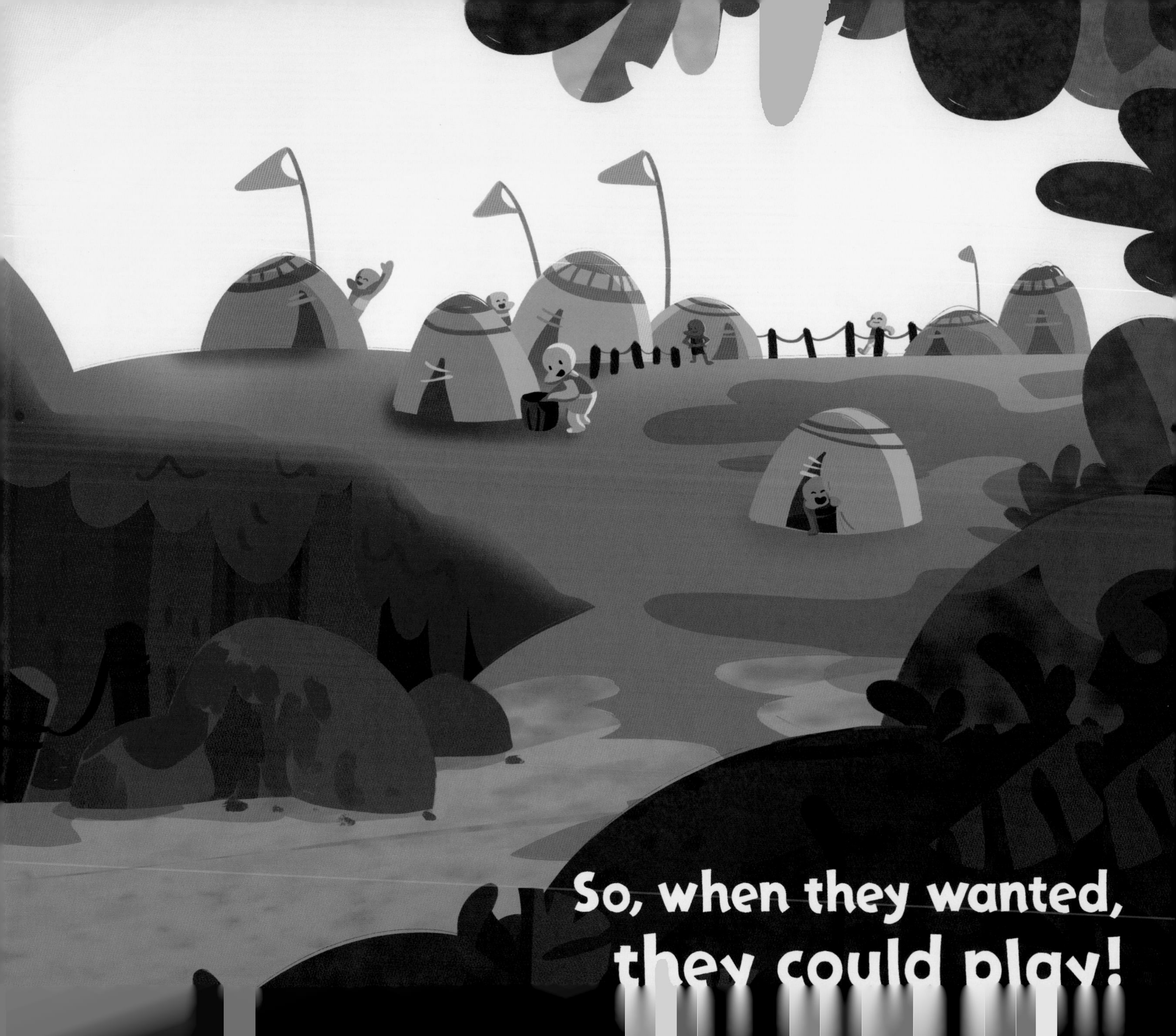

So, when they wanted,
they could play!

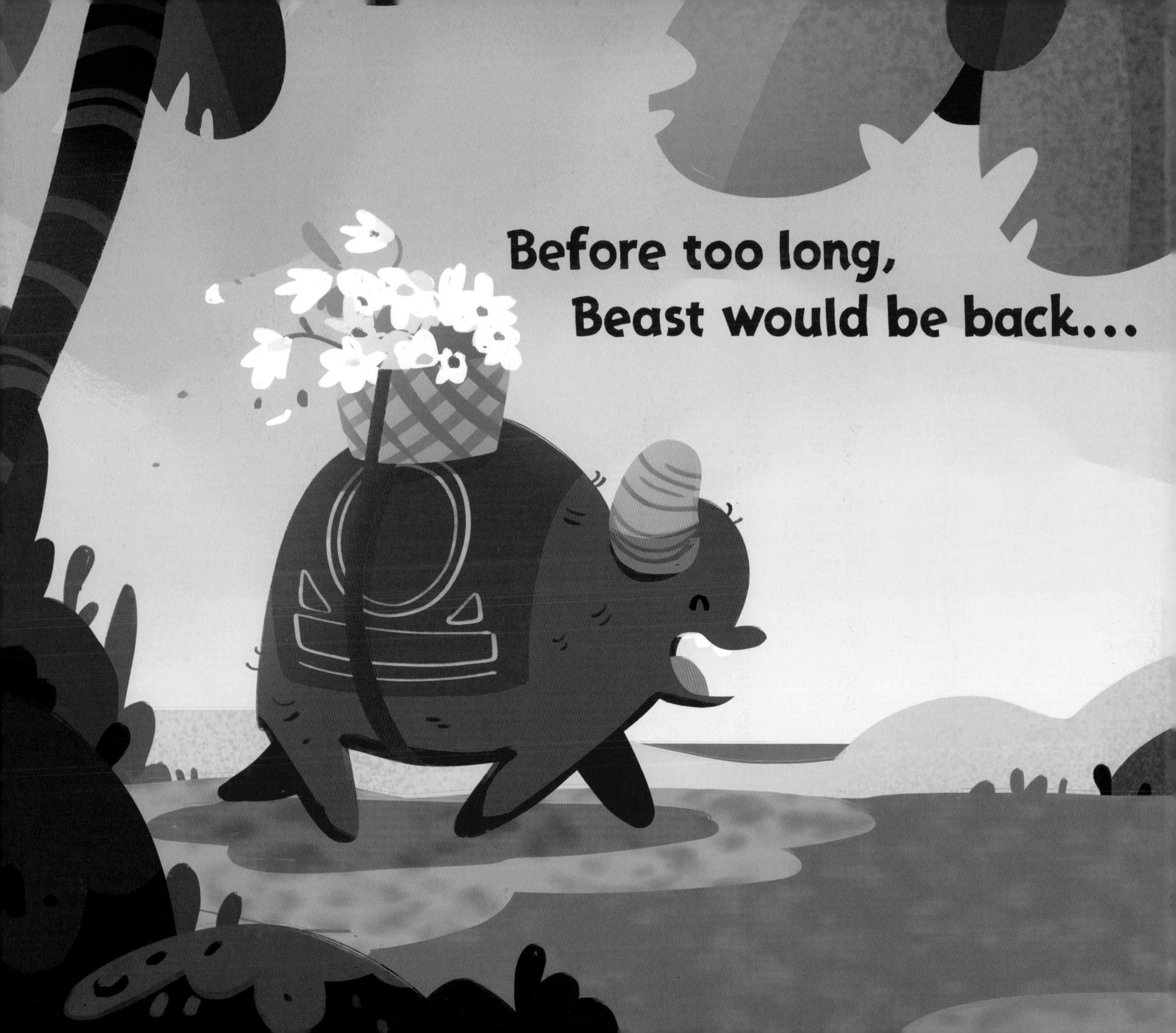

Before too long,
Beast would be back...

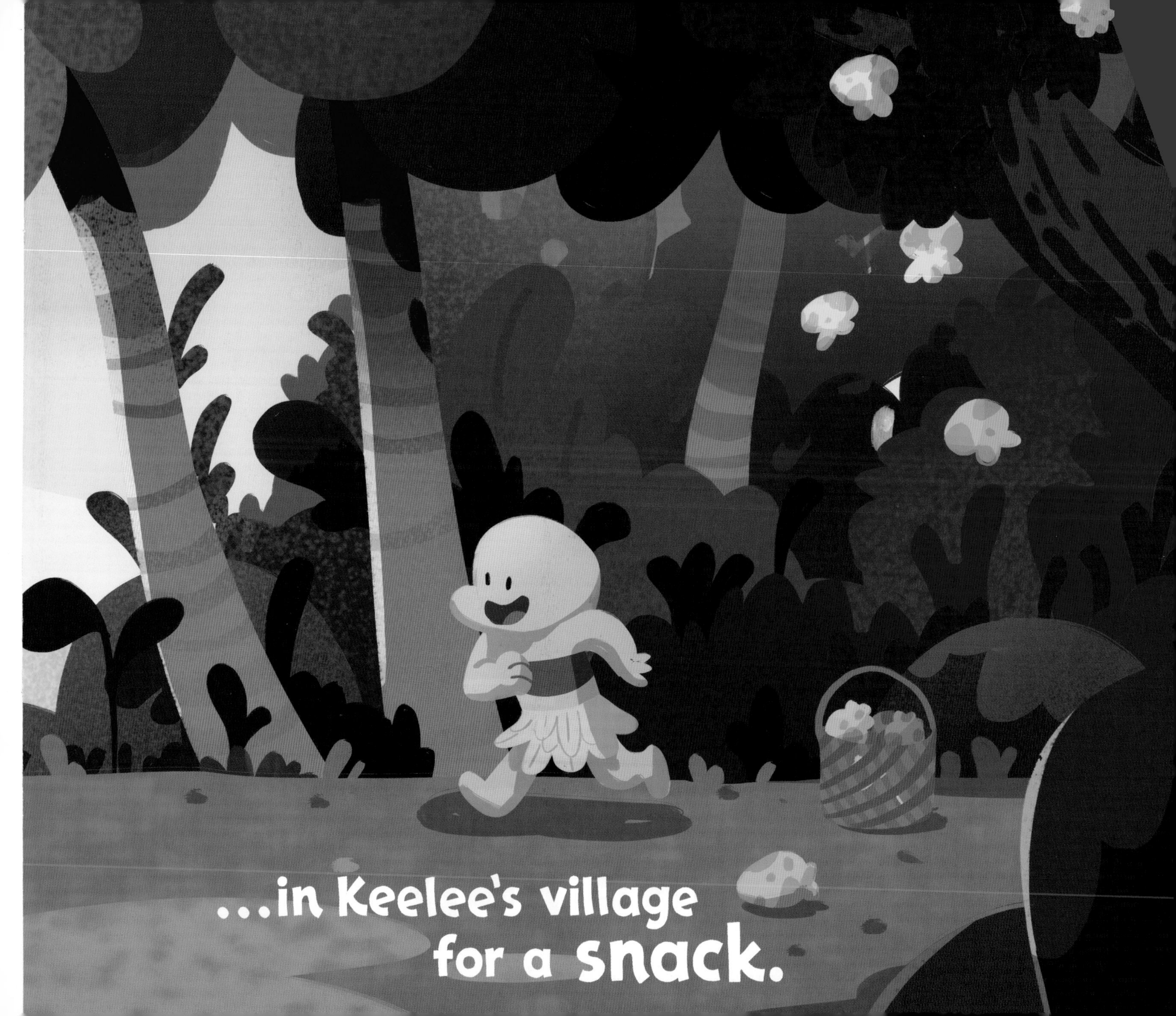

...in Keelee's village
for a **snack.**

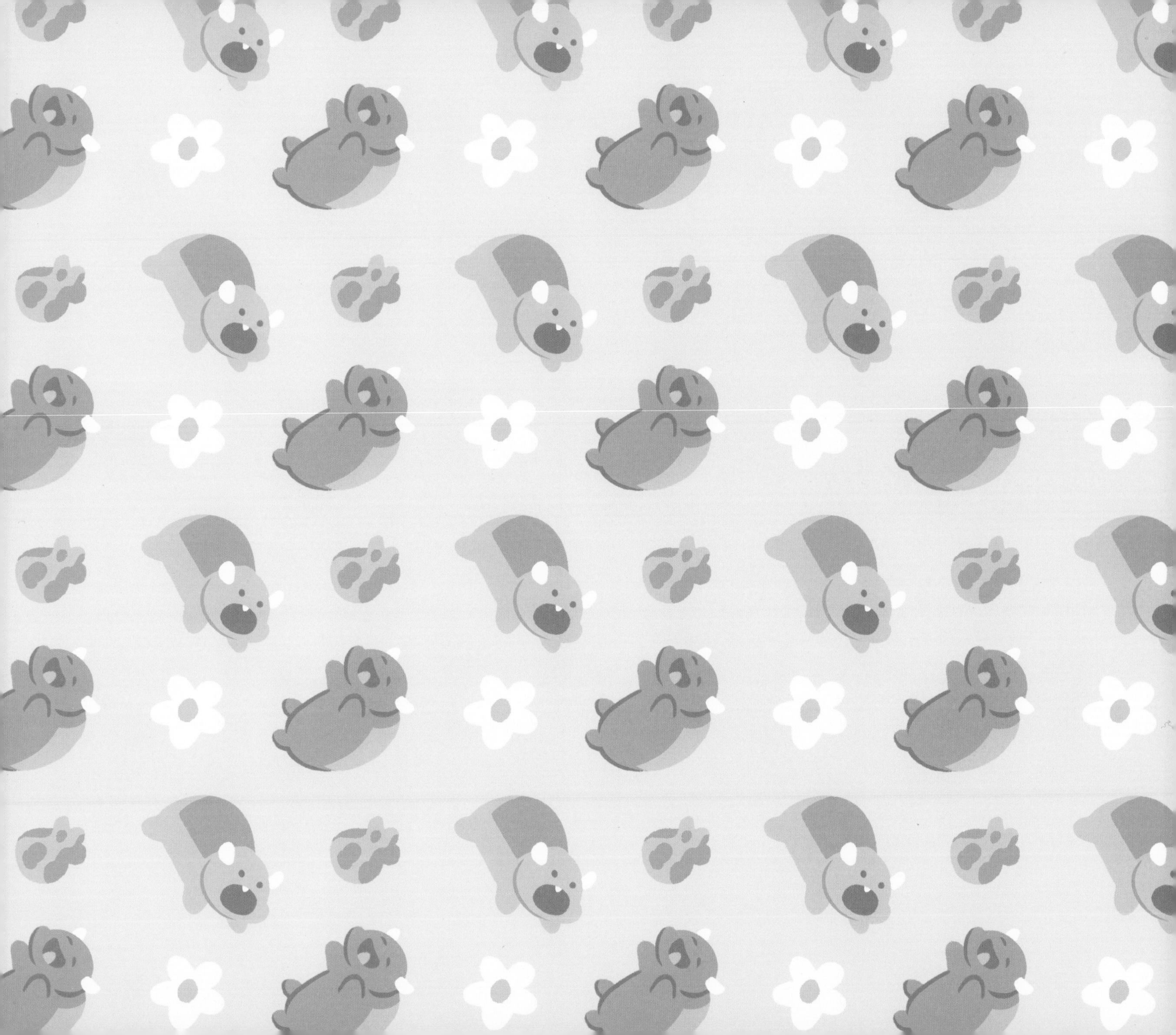